The
Upside
of
Ordinary

Susan
Lubner

Holiday House / New York

Library of Congress Cataloging-in-Publication Data

Lubner, Susan.

The upside of ordinary / by Susan Lubner. — 1st ed.

p. cm.

Summary: Eleven-year-old Jermaine's quest for fame as the creator of a reality television show based on her less-than-exciting family and friends teaches her important lessons about unbridled ambition, selfishness, and the upside of ordinary.

ISBN 978-0-8234-2417-7 (hardcover)

[1. Fame—Fiction. 2. Reality television programs—Fiction. 3. Family life— Fiction. 4. Humorous stories.] I. Title.

PZ7.L9682Up 2012

[E]—dc23

2011050563

For my father, the late Herbert C. Emple

ACKNOWLEDGMENTS

A special thank-you to Susan D. Jones of Root Cellar Preserves, for sharing your pickle-making know-how with me, and for the best sweet and spicy pickles on the planet; to Ari Buchler, Richard Braverman, and Al Miller, for your expert insight and advice; and to lovely Aunt Jean, the original balloon lady. Thanks for letting me dress up like a clown and sing happy birthday.

I am enormously grateful to all the extraordinary people at Holiday House, most especially to Sylvie Frank for your kind consideration and to Julie Amper, my far-from-ordinary editor, for your super keen eye, dedication, and guidance.

To my husband, David, and my daughters, Hannah and Julia, you are my heart and inspire me every day.

And to my "girls" Beth Raisner Glass, Patty Bovie, and Susan Lynn Meyer. Thank you for your constant support and friendship.

CONTENTS

The cheer from the audience was loud.

It felt like I was wearing it, as if it was a fancy winter coat, warm and special.

I tipped my face toward the pink stage lights above me.

Then in a quick swoop, I bowed so deeply my hair touched the stage floor.

I'll never forget how that cheer made me feel; important and shiny.

And I knew in that moment that someday, somehow, I would be famous.

1

Popcorn

A big THANK YOU to Dad and the super-pro vacuum he ordered on the internet. The huge carton it arrived in yesterday is just my size.

Through the little peephole I made in one of the cardboard walls, I film my sister Zelda eating leftover lasagna for breakfast.

I zoom in on her face as she spoons a stack of cheesy noodles into her mouth, her eyes glued to the TV. On the screen, two girls argue and a bad word gets bleeped out.

"Ha! UNBLALEEVRABLE!" Zelda says with a stuffed face.

"Mom doesn't like us to watch this reality show," I say, popping up from inside the box.

"AAAAAHHHHHHHHHHH!" My sister screams. A hunk of curly pasta drops out of her mouth. Zelda coughs. "Are you trying to kill me?" she sputters. "I almost choked to death!"

"Sorry," I say, lifting my leg over the top of the box.

Zelda drops her plate onto the coffee table. It clanks against the wooden top, which makes a great sound effect. Susie shuffles over and gobbles up the rest, the tags on her collar clinking with every lick.

"You're not sorry!" Zelda sneers. "You're a sneaky, annoying GERM!"

I'm not really a *germ*. "Jerm" is short for Jermaine, my name. Out of context it sounds like another word for bacteria...gross...I know. But it's catchy, too...perfect for a famous person.

"You were great!" I tell Zelda. "The element of surprise works for you."

"Leave me alone!" she snaps. I follow her, filming the back of her head, as she stomps into the kitchen.

Five days ago I started filming the reality show I am making about my family. So far this is what I have for footage: Mom cleaning a chicken for dinner, and thirty minutes of her working up a sweat on the Stairmaster; Susie rolling over for a biscuit; Dad plunging a toilet, sweeping the garage, and grumbling that no one but him ever thinks to throw out the brown bananas. The best stuff I've filmed is of my cranky big sister, Zelda. I surprised her when she stepped out of the shower (though Mom made sure I erased it), I caught her hissy fit when she couldn't find one of her sneakers, and of course there's this morning's riveting moment when she spat out that forkful of lasagna. And I'm just getting started! My reality show will be hugely interesting, which will make me hugely famous. I plan to include the seven hamsters living under the Ping-Pong table in my basement, too. I didn't mean to have seven. I brought only one home from the pet store. But a week or so later, Bernie gave birth to six babies! Dad says we should change Bernie's name to Bernadette, but

I think her name works just fine. (Note to self: film the cleaning of the cages.)

Then there's the pickle-making side of my mom. Yes! She's *the* pickle lady. Nora's Pickles are available in lots of grocery stores all over the state of Maine. That makes her pretty cool! You'd think that would have made me a *little* famous—Jermaine Davidson, the offspring of the local pickle lady. It's not like Mom is Aunt Jemima or Betty Crocker, but *I* think she's the best pickle-maker in the world. The world just doesn't know that yet, so I plan to film her at work. A cooking segment—great footage! Most people have no idea how much slicing and dicing is involved in the pickle-making process. (Note to self: figure out product placement for the pickles to improve Mom's sales!)

I turn the camera on Dad when he strolls into the kitchen. Dad wears his pants a tad too high to be considered cool. That's fine. It's good to have a variety of characters and personalities for my reality show. He sees the pan of lasagna next to the cornflakes Mom had left out for us on her way to make pickles in the barn behind the house.

"Who's eating lasagna for breakfast?" he asks. "Lasagna is not for breakfast!" Dad slides the lasagna back into the fridge. Then he opens the pantry door and rearranges the cereal boxes according to height, tallest on the left to shortest on the right, returning the cornflakes somewhere in the middle. Dad moves a can of soup back over to the "soup" side of the shelf.

"What's this doing here?" he asks nobody. He turns a few cans of vegetables label-side out before he shuts the door. "Who's going to help me wash the car?"

"I'm busy," Zelda says right away.

"It's too cold," I say.

"It's perfect car-washing weather!" Dad squints out the window at the bird-shaped thermometer. "It's already 40 degrees." He smiles.

Dad washes his car every Saturday. If it's *freezing* cold he'll drive it through a car wash, otherwise he'll do it by hand. Zelda says Dad is such a neat freak because his job as a pharmacist is so boring. "He counts hundreds of pills every day of his life. Of course washing his car and cleaning out the garage seem exciting," she pointed out.

Through the lens of my camera I double-check the mercury on the bird.

"Actually, Dad, the temperature is thirty-nine degrees. It's supposed to snow later today." Dad spots the dog-licked lasagna plate on the coffee table. A stray dish getting Dad in a twist will make for some nice drama. I zoom in.

"Who left that plate there?" he asks.

Hoping for another round of conflict, I rat out my sister. "Zelda."

"I'm not going to leave it there," she assures him.

"Please rinse it before it goes in the dishwasher," he tells her. The plate looks perfectly clean. And Dad doesn't look too ruffled. "I'm going to wash the car," he says. "Feel free to help. I'd enjoy the company."

After Dad leaves, Zelda opens the pantry and takes out some popcorn. She puts the flat packet into the microwave and closes the door.

Zelda punches the numbers on the panel but accidently sets the timer for thirty minutes instead of three! I decide to keep that mistake to myself. Both of us stand in front of the glass door waiting and watching as the bag grows bigger and bigger. I focus on the expanding bag.

"This is a long three minutes," Zelda says just as I smell smoke. I glance at the timer counting backward. It says

22 minutes and 36 seconds remaining. Zelda seems to notice the timer, too. Just as she says, "Whoops," the bag bursts into flames. Whoa...and I was just hoping for an *exploding* bag of popcorn!

Black smoke fills the microwave. The smoke alarm starts wailing. Susie barks and runs out of the room.

"Get Dad!" Zelda shouts at me, but I'm too busy filming the blaze, which is poking out the sides of the microwave door. The alarm is screeching. Zelda darts around looking for the portable phone, which is never where it's supposed to be. "Call 911!" she screams.

"Yes! Do that!" I order her. *Let's get some firemen in the scene!* But before either of us can find a phone, Dad practically flies into the kitchen with soap bubbles on his sleeves. He flings open a cabinet door, grabs a box of baking soda, and throws the white powder at the flames. It snuffs out the fire. The popcorn bag is completely charred, and so is the inside of the microwave.

"You could have burned the house down!" Dad says, panting. "Who's eating popcorn for breakfast?" he frantically asks us. "Popcorn is not for breakfast!"

My camera continues to roll: incinerated popcorn, and Dad flipping his lid. That's exactly the kind of footage that makes for great reality TV. So awesome, it's sure to put me on the map.

Here I come, world!

2
Scrabble

Before I got the idea to make a reality-TV show, I was already planning to become a star. Ever since my huge success playing Pinocchio in the school play last month I could not stop thinking about all the clapping and cheering from the audience when I took my final bow. I felt *shiny*. It's no wonder famous people are called stars. I decided right then and there that I would become famous. Limo-riding, camera-flashing, crowd-cheering famous!

So I made a list of ways to make that happen:

~~Movie star~~
~~Supermodel~~

Being a movie star was my number one choice. But I'd need to get to Hollywood. My parents would never move to Hollywood. They're totally un-Californian—especially Dad. I'd have to wait until I was old enough to get my own apartment, and I'm in too much of a hurry for that.

The supermodel option was really just wishful thinking. Let's face it, how many supermodels can you think of that have frizzy brown hair and a palate expander? Even my Magic 8 Ball said *"Don't count on it"* when I asked it for advice.

So why the reality show? Here's how it all started.

A few days before I figured out how to launch myself to stardom, Mom had dropped my best friend, Nina; Zelda; and me off at the Bluebird Nest & Rest Senior Home where we often visit Nina's granny, Viola Church, and spend time with the other residents. We were supposed to play bingo with the old folks, but most of them fell asleep around the table, and Granny V had a hard time remembering the numbers, even with our help. So we wheeled her into the TV room and watched *Who Wants to Marry the Rock Star.* When Mom returned and saw us watching TV, and Granny V snoring in her wheelchair, she was miffed with a capital M.

"This is a far cry from bingo!" she said just as the TV bleeped out a bad word. "Where is Pat?" she asked, referring to the nurse's aide. Mom's not too keen on reality shows (though she and Dad will admit *So You Want to Be a Pastry Chef, Dance 'til You Drop,* and *Real or Toupee* are "harmless fun" and "family-appropriate").

"They should make a show about kids who study hard and read a lot," Mom said to us when we left the rest home.

"Watching someone read is boring," I said.

"There's no value in that rock-star show! It's shocking!" she continued. I could see her point. Thirty women compete to be the bride, and they can be nasty!

"That's true," I admitted, "but sometimes it's fun to be shocked."

Here's one shock I didn't like. At the dinner table that

night Mom announced, "Your father and I have decided that both of you are watching too much television. From now on," she sang, "Sunday night is family game night!"

Zelda gasped like she'd seen a ghost. "*Game* night?"

Mom wasn't kidding. That Sunday, a mere three days after her game-night proclamation, we played Scrabble. But it turned out to be a good thing! That's when I figured out *how* I was going to become famous.

"Let's keep a list of unfamiliar words that are spelled out tonight," Dad suggested.

"Yes," Mom said. "You kids can look up the definitions, and we can put together our own *Davidson Dictionary*!"

"Scrabble is a terrific way to improve your vocabulary!" Dad said.

"*Fart*," Zelda said, laying her letters out in a row.

"I think you can do better than that," my father scolded.

"It's a real word! Look it up!" she protested. At that point, Mom leaned over to double-check Zelda's letters.

"Ooh, ooh, look, Zel!" Mom bounced excitedly in her seat. She was frantically pointing her finger. "You can spell *farthest* and get an extra fifty points for using all seven letters!"

"Hey, not fair! You're helping her!" I complained.

"I'm trying to prove a point," my mother said. "Your sister's word is offensive."

"What's so offensive about *fart*? Susie does it all the time and you don't give her grief!" Zelda argued.

"Susie is a dog and doesn't know about good manners!" Mom pointed out. "We should have a rule about which words are not allowed."

"You can't change the rules of Scrabble! What are you, the word police?" Zelda was fuming.

"Let's play, for heaven's sake!" Dad said.

My mind started to wander. I thought about dessert because I hadn't had any. That reminded me of Pudding Cakes...a new snack Nina had packed in her lunch. School lunch reminded me of school and that I had forgotten to practice my math facts. Then I started thinking that I would be too tired to practice my math facts anyway and what I really wanted to do was leave this Scrabble game and go watch TV.

Suddenly Zelda flew out of her chair and screamed, "I quit!"

Dad jumped up, too. His lips puckered and twisted like they were trying to fit over the right-sized words.

"Sit back down!" he managed to growl, his arms flailing above his head. "We're having some quality family time!"

Zelda glared at him. "I'm being forced to use her words!" She pointed at my mother. "I'm not playing if she's going to choose words for me!"

"I was helping!" Mom squawked in surprise. "Not *forcing*...suggesting!" Mom rearranged her tiles on her letter rack. I saw that she had the *Z*, which was worth a whopping ten points all by itself.

I quickly concluded that watching Zelda fight with my parents over the word *fart* was actually better than watching television...which made me think of reality TV because really, reality TV is the ultimate eavesdropping experience! Who doesn't feel a secret thrill listening in on a heated conversation? Show me a person who doesn't delight in flabbergasting surprises—like overhearing your teacher mumble a swear word (which really happened to me), or discovering that your mom's friend has a patch of hair growing under her chin (I won't say which friend).

It's shocking, fascinating, freaky, sometimes all at once. That's reality TV. And we can gawk, gasp, and snicker in the comfort of our own homes.

And then these thoughts swelled into one giant idea, like a tidal wave, splitting open like the Red Sea, TA DA! A wide-open path to fame!

"I'm going to make a reality-TV show!" I announced. Everyone stopped arguing. "It's going to be about our family," I continued excitedly. But even as those words tumbled off my tongue I was thinking... *I'll download my show onto the web! Post it right on one of those sites where everyone can watch it... like Spyonme.com.*

"Guess what?" Mom said. "I think it's a great idea!"

"You do?" my father asked.

"*Making* a TV show means using your brain," Mom continued. "And anything that uses the brain and is creative, I like." Mom leaned over and squeezed my arm.

"What are you going to do with your show when you finish it?" Dad asked. My churning brain must have created some static electricity. Other thoughts kept clinging to it. Like, why limit my fame potential to cyberspace junkies? Why not aim for the stars—I'd be just like Rufus Carmichael, the famous reality-show producer! He's become a *huge* celebrity by hosting some of his own shows! My show doesn't need a host... but it is about *my* family. It makes perfect sense for me to appear on camera, too! I bet Rufus Carmichael will help me get it aired on national TV! He could take credit for discovering me—the first eleven-year-old reality-show prodigy! I'd probably have to take a limo to school since everyone would fight over who got to sit with me on the bus.

"Oh it's just for fun, Clark!" Mom said, interrupting my thoughts. "Jermaine is experimenting. She can have a special family showing when she's finished. An ordinary, Scrabble-playing family is a fine example of reality TV," she chirped.

"Rrrright," I said. But a family showing wouldn't do, and neither would ordinary—not if I wanted to be famous.

In reality (no pun intended), I had much bigger plans.

3
Reality Check

Dear Mr. Carmichael,

Tonight, right in the middle of a heated game of Scrabble, I decided to produce a reality-TV show about my family! I have watched some of your shows and I think they are A-M-A-Z-I-N-G! I've never seen Outlaws *because my parents say it's inappropriate. But I love* The Country Life. *Maybe you could come film that show in my town? We have a barn and everything—no cows, though, just pickles. But it's pretty country-like out here. Maybe we could work together? You could film me filming my family. FYI I have a hotheaded thirteen-year-old sister who would provide some awesome material. Plus it would be a great way for me to get my show on TV.*

Filming starts tomorrow right after school. Lights, camera, action! (HA! How do I sound?) I'd really appreciate any tips you could give me on reality-show production. I am new at this.

Thank you.

Yours truly,
Jermaine Davidson

PS Have you Googled yourself? There are millions of news articles and photos of you. You are extremely famous. I want to be extremely famous, too!

4
Red, White, and Blue

I prop the camera on the counter so I can film Zelda and me scrubbing the charred microwave clean. It takes about twenty minutes. There's still a bit of black stuff and a melted spot that we label permanent damage. Dad tries to get what's left with a Brillo pad.

"You need to be more careful," he says.

"Sorry." I cringe when I think of what could have happened.

"Next time, try a bowl of cereal for breakfast," Dad says.

"I wasn't the one who wanted popcorn," I explain.

"You're the one who stood around filming while the house was on fire!" Zelda argues.

Dad tips his head and raises his eyebrows at us as if to say, *You're both at fault.*

Mom comes in through the back door. Her cheeks are flushed from the chilly air. She swings her bright green Nora's Pickles tote bag off her shoulder, catching the bottom with her other hand. Then she pulls out a jar of piccalilli and two jars of dills and plunks them onto the counter.

"I've got so much to do for the Winter Pickle Palooza," she says. Then she sniffs. "What burned?"

"I'm surprised you didn't hear the smoke alarm," Dad says.

"I can't hear anything in that barn with the sink spraying and the dishwasher running." Sticking out from under her bulky knit hat, a puff of red hair hugs each side of her jaw. "It stinks in here, what happened?" she asks again. Dad explains about the popcorn and the fire.

"My goodness! I'm glad the house is still standing and everyone's okay. I guess I missed all the excitement. Speaking of excitement..." Mom cranks a window open to help diffuse the smell. "Brrrrr." She shivers. "We're going to Edie and Larry's tonight for a Fourth of July dinner party!"

"In February?" Zelda whines.

"That's the whole idea! It's supposed to snow later on. What better way to get through a cold, snowy winter than by having a big summer blowout?" Mom smiles.

"Strange," Dad says, shaking his head. But I'm thinking *YAHOOO!* Aunt Edie and Uncle Larry are fun. What a great way to spice up my reality show! The last themed dinner was dead-presidents night. The centerpiece on the table, made out of a shoebox, was a mini version of Ford's Theatre where Abraham Lincoln was shot. How brilliant is that? Clay headstones were propped up against the dinner plates, each with a dead president's name etched into it. Mine said John Adams even though I was dressed as George Washington. Dessert was a White House cake with black frosting. Uncle Larry was John F. Kennedy.

Even though Uncle Larry has the thickest Maine accent of anyone I know, he adjusted it just enough to sound like he might have been from Boston. The night was awesome and typically weird.

Back when my cousin Melinda was a baby, Uncle Larry and Aunt Edie lived in a camper. Not one of those gigantic bus-like things, but a pop-up one that they hitched to the back of their car. "Why live in a house, when there's a whole wide world out there?" Uncle Larry still likes to say. Too bad they live in a house now. The pop-up-camper angle would have added another dimension to my show. Like a road show! Now the camper sits lopsided in the driveway with a flat tire.

Uncle Larry likes to invent things. He once made a T-shirt to fit over a tissue box. It came in different colors and said *Achoo!* on one side and *Bless you* on the other. I thought it was a great idea. He and Aunt Edie tried to sell them at craft fairs, but nobody wanted to shell out money for a T-shirt for their tissues. And nobody wanted disposable cooking utensils that kept catching on fire, either. Then there was the automatic door stopper (it didn't stop any doors but made plenty of holes in the wall), the Svelte Belt, which was supposed to help you lose weight but gave you indigestion instead, and a bunch of other stuff that didn't do what it was supposed to do. Uncle Larry says one of these days he'll invent something that will make him rich. Then he'll hook up that old camper, and they can travel the whole country. (Of course if he gets rich, he'll probably buy a new camper.)

For now, Aunt Edie and Uncle Larry run a balloon business. Besides selling giant turkey balloons on Thanksgiving and three-foot pumpkin balloons on Halloween, Aunt Edie and Uncle Larry dress up in costumes and deliver balloon-a-grams to their customers. Sometimes Melinda, Zelda, and I get to help at special events. On our birthdays, we get the balloon animal of our choice. Uncle Larry makes unbelievable two-hump camels.

At six o'clock we head over to my aunt and uncle's house for the Fourth of July dinner. I capture the ride with my camera. It's snowing, and the streets are like white ribbons stretched out in front of us. The frozen Kenduskeag stream will have to wait until the spring thaw before it can empty itself into the river at the other end of Bangor. It shadows the road until we cross the bridge into town, and then it disappears.

Dad makes a turn after the Copper Kettle Diner. The sign in the window says OPEN in red neon letters. There's a man stomping the snow off his boots in the doorway.

The Bluebird Nest & Rest Senior Home is lit up inside. I see the flash of a TV screen when we pass by. I imagine Granny V with her frayed afghan tucked around her, watching reruns of *Murder She Wrote*. Her tired feet snug in moccasins, underneath pale blue ankles, pressed against the metal footrests of her wheelchair.

The short ride takes longer than it normally does because my mother is a nervous wreck about crashing.

"Slow down, Clark. The roads look treacherous," she keeps repeating.

"I'm creeping as it is, Nora," he replies each time.

I stop my camera because it's so repetitive it will bore the viewers.

When we arrive at my aunt and uncle's house I turn the camera back on. A red, white, and blue balloon arch frames the doorway to the kitchen, and several shiny star-shaped balloons float across the ceiling.

Mom brings creamed-corn casserole because good corn on the cob is hard to get this time of year. She pulls the foil back so I can zoom in on the bread-crumb topping. Dad carries in piccalilli and the two jars of pickles.

"Juggle!" I tell him.

"I can't do that. I'm not a good juggler."

"Try! Please!" I beg. I already know he can't juggle, which is the whole point. I aim the camera at Dad.

"Jermaine, don't be ridiculous. I don't think Aunt Edie would appreciate me repainting the hallway with pickle juice."

"Fine." I sigh, knowing that he's right.

On our way to the kitchen we pass through the dining room. I pan the camera around. The usual mismatched seats have been replaced with folding lawn chairs, and the table is covered in a red checkered cloth made out of plastic. In the center is a bunch of balloons tied to a large silver bell with *Liberty* written across it in black marker. Leaning up against the bell is the Declaration of Independence stapled to a piece of scroll-shaped Styrofoam with a feathered pen sticking out of the side. On each dinner plate is a plastic flag held upright by a little blue ball. I pick up one of the flags and sniff at the handmade stand. I thought so. Play-Doh. My cousin's cat, Louise, jumps up to eat the ribbon hanging from one of the balloons.

"Shooo! Get off of there, Louise!" my father hisses. "There goes my appetite," he mumbles. I hear Aunt Edie's voice boom from the kitchen.

"THREE CHEERS FOR THE RED, WHITE, AND BLUE—THE ARMY AND NAVY FOREEEEEEEVER!" Aunt Edie marches in place in front of the stove. Because the grill outside is covered in a mound of snow, she boils hot dogs. She pokes at them with a long fork. I zoom in on the American-flag earrings that swing from her ears. Dad rolls his eyes.

"Don't be a stick-in-the-mud!" Mom whispers to him. "Hello, everybody," Mom calls cheerfully.

"Happy birthday, fellow patriots!" Aunt Edie greets us. "Oh, you brought a video camera! What a smart idea! We never take ours out, do we, Larry?"

My uncle is counting hot-dog buns and placing them in a basket. "I think it's been ten years since we used it," he tells us. "Melinda was just a year old."

I scan my camera over to the boiling water on the burner. The pink ends of the hot dogs poke through the bubbles, rising above the rim of the pot. "Smile, Aunt Edie!" I say.

"Jermaine is making a reality show about our family," Mom announces. I catch her wink at Aunt Edie on camera.

"No kidding!" Aunt Edie says. "Don't get a close-up of me. I haven't waxed my mustache in a month."

"Cool, a reality show! Can I be in it?" my cousin Melinda asks. She's wearing a bikini, her pale skin looking almost ghostly under the kitchen light, and a fake tattoo on each forearm, *Peace Baby* on one and a black and white yin-yang on the other.

"Of course, you're all going to be in it!" Melinda steps right in front of the camera. I zoom out so I can film more than her left cheek.

"Too bad we have the most boring family on the planet," Zelda interrupts. Then she closes her eyes and starts to snore.

"Zelda," Mom chides. "We are anything but boring!" Zelda tips her head back and snores louder. The phone rings.

"I've got it." Uncle Larry almost trips sprinting to

snatch it up. Aunt Edie looks over her shoulder. Uncle Larry speaks softly.

"Who's that calling?" Aunt Edie asks.

"Balloon order." Uncle Larry hangs up.

"A good one, I hope." Edie turns around to face Larry.

"It's . . . for tonight," Uncle Larry says slowly.

"Tonight? It's already tonight!" Aunt Edie yelps. "Did you tell them we need at least twenty-four hours notice for orders?" Uncle Larry turns away when he answers.

"It's all right. I'll take care of it. It's just a simple birthday bouquet. The girls can help blow up the balloons."

"Hmmm . . ." Edie says, and turns back to the pot of hot dogs. "So long as you don't need to deliver in the middle of our dinner," she tells him.

"Not a problem," he assures her. Louise jumps up onto the counter next to Aunt Edie.

"Oh, for Pete's sake," my father moans. "Do you know where her feet have been?"

"I heard that cats are cleaner than humans," I tell him.

"Not cleaner than Dad," Zelda says.

"I don't know *any* humans who stand around in litter boxes and walk all over kitchen counters and tables," my father argues.

"Girls, take Louise upstairs," Aunt Edie tells us. "She doesn't seem to understand the dangers of a hot stove."

Melinda scoops the cat up and holds her over her shoulder. For a split second I imagine Louise's tail going up in smoke. But I push that awful thought out of my brain. Poor Louise! Plus I already have the microwave fire in my show. I need more variety. I am following Zelda and Melinda out of the kitchen when Louise gags and coughs up a hunk of something red. I film a stream of yellow liquid running out of the cat's mouth and a red glob falling to the floor.

"Ewww!" Zelda yells. "Louise coughed up part of her gut."

"Where?" Melinda spins around, still holding Louise. "What is that?" she squeals. Though a gut would have been much more exciting, I'm glad to see it's definitely not.

"Are you okay, Louise?" I ask. "It's just a piece of red ribbon." I zoom in on it.

"Oh my gosh, did she barf on me?" Melinda freezes. "I'm going to be sick!" Aunt Edie rushes over with a wad of paper towels. She inspects Melinda's shoulder.

"You're fine, honey," she tells Melinda. "It's just a little mess on the floor. What happened, sweetie?" she coos at the cat.

"That's good," Melinda says. She strokes the top of Louise's head.

Okay, this isn't so bad—gross, but it's a start, I tell myself. Who knows what else she might puke up...maybe a whole mouse! That would be interesting!

On the way up to Melinda's room I grab a can of lemonade from the ice-filled rubber blow-up pool next to the staircase. Then I aim my camera at the striped cat still slung over my cousin's shoulder, and hope for the best.

5
Icy

The lawn chairs we sit in at the dinner table are low, and we have to raise our arms a bit to reach our plates. We look like a family of dwarves. But it's easy to film while we eat, since it's basically a one-handed meal. I'm glad we're not having steak or barbequed chicken, because it would be impossible to hold my camera if I had to use a knife and fork.

"Speaking of balloon deliveries, when are you getting the second delivery van?" Dad asks.

"The beginning of the week," Aunt Edie says excitedly. "We saw an ad in the paper for a used one in great condition. Once we have it, we should be able to double our deliveries." I point the camera at Uncle Larry, who is shaking his head.

"I still say the best way to increase our business is efficiency. The faster we can put together balloon orders, the more orders we can handle," he says. I zoom in as Uncle Larry pushes half a hot dog into his mouth.

"Oh—are you thinking of hiring someone to help out?" Mom asks. Uncle Larry shakes his head and wipes the side of his face with a napkin.

"We can't afford that," Aunt Edie says. "We barely have enough for the down payment on the van."

"I have something else in mind," Uncle Larry says, his mouth still full.

"We are not discussing *that*!" Aunt Edie snaps. *"That"* blows angrily across the table, like an airborne exclamation mark, and seems to smack Uncle Larry right between the eyes. He stops chewing and his eyebrows hunch up like two furry caterpillars. My aunt and uncle glare at each other without saying a word. I feel a pinch of excitement that a big fight is brewing. I aim the camera at my uncle.

"Would someone please pass Nora's piccalilli?" Dad smiles at my mom. "Does anyone want more corn stuff?" he asks.

"It's a casserole," Mom corrects him. "By the way, did you all know that the Liberty Bell supposedly got that crack the very first time it was rung?" I am peeved that my parents try to head off the battle between my aunt and uncle, who are still staring each other down. It works, too. Aunt Edie looks away and holds her plate out to Mom, who spoons on a small pile of corn casserole. Uncle Larry finishes off the rest of his hot dog.

People around here should let nature take its course so I can get some action for my show. What would Rufus Carmichael do?

Still holding my camera, I stretch across the table as if I am reaching for the ketchup. I bump the pitcher of ice water that is conveniently close to my arm. It lands in my mother's lap.

"ARGGGGGGGHHHH!" Mom jumps out of her seat like a broken spring and the glass pitcher rolls off her lap and smashes with a loud crash. Water gushes down the front of her Bermudas and ice cubes scatter and slide all over the place like loose marbles. I stop filming for a second. I didn't plan for that to happen! I was just hoping for a harmless spill.

"Mom! Are you okay?" I look over at Mom's dripping legs. No blood. Phew! I restart my camera and catch Aunt Edie running to the kitchen. She brings back a stack of dish towels covered with plaid roosters. Dad grabs the towels from Aunt Edie and carefully mops up the floor, trying to avoid the shattered glass.

"Bring a broom and dustpan!" Uncle Larry yells. I zoom in on Dad as he drops towels over the mini lake running under the table.

"Are you cut, Nora?" Dad asks.

"No, just freezing. May I have one of those towels, please?" Mom shivers just as Dad drops the last one on top of the icy mess. I get up from my seat so that I can get Dad on all fours. "Can I get a towel, *please*?" Mom asks. Aunt Edie leaves the room again and Dad smacks his head on the table as he tries to stand back up. The silverware rattles from the jolt and Dad says a swear word. Yes! I will have a bleep in my show!

"Jermaine!" Dad hollers when he notices me with the camera. "Put that camera down and go get a towel for your mother."

"Okay, I will. Hang on just one second." My poor mother is freezing. But the footage is so much better than a barfing cat.

"Jermaine!" Mom scolds. I shut the camera off.

"I'm going," I say, but Aunt Edie has already returned

with a bath towel and a pair of pants for my mother. She has a small broom and dustpan tucked under her arm. Uncle Larry is working on something stuck between his front teeth as he pushes one of the rooster towels around with his foot. Then he bends down and carefully gathers the large pieces of broken glass. My sister and cousin are still seated at the table.

"You kids better stay put," Uncle Larry orders. "I don't want any of you stepping on glass. It's all over the place," he warns. My mom's shorts are plastered to her legs and drops of water make a *tap, tap* sound as they hit the floor.

"That includes you, Miss Movie Maker," Dad barks, "who by the way won't be filming any more scenes at the dinner table."

"It's not a movie, it's a reality show," I correct him. But I don't blame him for being mad. "Sorry, Mom," I say, sitting back down at the table. "Sorry I broke your pitcher, Aunt Edie, and for the mess."

"It was an accident, Jermaine," she says to me. I feel myself blush. "And it's just water," my aunt continues. "In this family we don't cry over spilled milk, and we won't cry over spilled water—even if it's freezing cold, poor Nora."

"I owe you a pitcher," Mom says.

"No, Jermaine does," Zelda says.

"Oh, I think I paid two dollars for that thing at a yard sale. I don't care about the pitcher, I'm just glad no one got cut on the glass." Unfolding the towel, she wraps it around my mother's waist.

After apple pie à la mode, we play a couple of games of rubber horseshoes in the hallway. Then Zelda, Melinda, and I help Uncle Larry.

At the back of the house, in a spare bedroom, is the headquarters for the balloon business. There are two large tanks of helium in the corner of the room and dozens of white plastic storage bins, each holding several bags of rubber balloons that have been sorted by color and size. The shiny Mylar balloons are stacked on shelves, separated into thin piles of *Happy Birthday*, *It's a Boy!* (or girl), *Get Well Soon*, and others for assorted happy and not-so-happy occasions. Several colorful spools of ribbon spread across a long table like a rainbow, and a pair of scissors hangs from a small hook nailed into the wall. I film a few moments of Zelda and Melinda inflating balloons. I'm feeling excited about the scene I shot at dinner—okay, and a little guilty, too. But "orchestrating" a few more scenes like that will definitely make my show more interesting. Placing the camera on one of the shelves, I film us helping out.

I slip the neck of a balloon onto one of the helium tanks. I lift up the tip of the valve and a whooshing noise escapes. The balloon expands into a large red tulip.

"Who are these balloons for, anyway?" Melinda asks.

"Someone at the Bluebird Nest & Rest Senior Home is celebrating her ninety-third birthday," Uncle Larry answers. He supervises us for a few more minutes. His thinning hair is full of static and it floats up from his head, swaying back and forth. It's almost nine o'clock when we finish the bouquet and Uncle Larry leaves to put on his costume. When he comes back wearing his feathery penguin suit, I film him waddling across the room, the black swim fins that he wears for penguin feet tucked under his arm for later. Uncle Larry waves a black-and-white wing at the camera. He pokes his arms out of the armholes underneath, and blows a kiss. I imagine myself blowing kisses into a camera. I'm wearing a dress that swishes and really big earrings. A crowd chants my name, "Jermaine, Jermaine..."

"Jermaine, hello...Earth to Jermaine." Uncle Larry pokes his beak against my cheek.

"Can I have those now?" He reaches for the bouquet of balloons I hold in my other hand. Still in a daze, I think about those oversized earrings as Uncle Larry shuffles out the back door.

Only when I hear the old, beat-up delivery van thunder down the road do I remember that at the Bluebird Nest & Rest Senior Home, the lights go out at eight o'clock.

6
Sorry to Bother You Again, Mr. Carmichael, But...

Dear Mr. Carmichael,

How do you make sure your shows never get a little boring? Since my family is sort of ordinary (totally ordinary is more like it) I figure if I want to be famous like you, I need to find a way to kick my show up a notch. I've been focusing more on directing. I think it's called stage-directing or staging? I "set up" some of the drama. Do you think that's a good idea? It's not like cheating, is it? If you could let me know if I am on the right track, I would really appreciate it.

Hopefully you are getting my letters. I haven't heard back from you yet, but that's probably *because you are so busy. In the meantime I'll go with my gut feeling and keep "directing" my show more. My dad always says, "Take the bull by the horns!" I guess I'll take his advice. But I could really use some expert reality-show advice. Fast.*

Thank you.

Your biggest fan,
Jermaine Davidson

7

Missing

WHAT! The word vibrates inside my head and startles me awake. I freeze. My heart thumps inside me like it's trying to break out of my chest. I realize I'm holding my breath. My eyes try desperately to see in the dark. I am positive I heard someone say *WHAT!*

"How can that be?" I hear my mom's voice through the wall. I begin to relax. There's no ghost or murderer in my room. It's just the sound of my parents' voices drifting through my bedroom wall. My clock glows 5:07. I can tell by the speed and high pitch of the mumbled conversation that something isn't right. I sit up and listen. My mom sounds frantic. People don't have high-pitched conversations at five o'clock in the morning unless something is wrong. The room is dark and I feel for my camera, which I know is somewhere on the floor next to me. I find it and tiptoe out of my room and into the hallway. My parents' bedroom door is slightly open, and light spills in a pattern of squares in front of me. I carefully position the lens through the opening. Mom is pacing back and forth, and now of course I can hear everything.

"Where is he?" Dad stands in the middle of the room in his underwear, rubbing the back of his neck. Not a glamorous sight for national TV, I tell you.

"I—I—I don't know..." Mom stutters, holding the portable phone in her hand. Her springy hair sticks out all over the place. *Where's who?* I wonder.

"What did Edie say?" Dad asks.

"She didn't say much," Mom answers. "She doesn't know." Mom throws her hands into the air. "Larry called to say he was fine, and not to worry, and that was it!" *Uncle Larry? They're talking about Uncle Larry!* My heart starts thumping around again.

"That doesn't make sense," my father says, shaking his head.

"Of course it doesn't make sense! Does anything make sense with my sister and her husband?" Mom slaps her forehead, thankfully with the hand that isn't holding the phone. Well, actually, Mom knocking herself out by smacking the phone against her head would really be something to film. I push that thought away and concentrate on my parents' conversation. "She said that he promised everything was going to be fine and he'd be home very soon. And that's it," Mom tells Dad. I zoom in on her worried face.

Uncle Larry ran away? Why? I imagine him scurrying down the street, holding a small suitcase under his penguin wing.

"Well, what now?" Dad asks. "Should one of us go over there?"

"No. Edie doesn't want to risk Melinda waking up and getting upset. She hasn't figured out what to tell her. Edie doesn't know what to think herself." Mom sighs and plops down on the bed. Her freckled knees poke out from beneath the hem of her flannel nighty and she crosses her legs at the ankle. I feel a knot tightening in my chest when I think about Melinda.

"Well, he's all right at least. Physically, anyway." Dad sits next to Mom on the bed and pats her shoulder. *Physically?* I wonder. *As opposed to mentally? Did Uncle Larry have some type of breakdown?*

"Oh, I'm sure he's up to something," Mom says. Before I have a chance to wonder what that's supposed to mean, Mom jumps up from the bed. "I'm going to fold laundry."

"Now?" Dad asks. That's my cue to hightail it back to my room. I am just out of sight when my parents' bedroom door swings wide open. I keep the camera rolling. I can still record their voices.

"Yes, now. I can't sleep," Mom whispers so as not to wake us up.

I hear Dad go back inside the bedroom, and Mom's footsteps on the stairs. I shut the camera off and climb back into bed. Why would Uncle Larry want to run away? What about Melinda? And Aunt Edie? I bet it had something to do with the fight he had with Aunt Edie! I fold the top of my blankets up against my neck and flip over onto my side. My mind keeps playing back the Fourth of July dinner. Where was Uncle Larry *really* going with those balloons? I bet not the rest home. The old folks are in bed sleeping at eight o'clock. Then who was it that called on the phone earlier?

Sleep starts to interfere with my thoughts. My brain feels fuzzy. I see Uncle Larry on the telephone...then he waves goodbye. Is it Uncle Larry, or maybe it's somebody else? Waving...waving...to a huge crowd of people...the crowd waves back...they're waving at something...a giant penguin...no...somebody...somebody wearing a fancy dress...with big earrings and frizzy hair.

At breakfast, Mom and Dad tell us about Uncle Larry.

"He's gone on a trip for a while," Mom explains.

"That's weird." Zelda reaches across the table and swipes her knife across the butter. "He decided to take a trip in the middle of the night?" Zelda gives Mom a look that says *We're supposed to believe that?* Then she takes a big bite out of her bagel.

Mom plays with the colorful clay beads around her neck. She slides them back and forth over the leather cord. "I don't really know, Zelda," she admits.

"Well, is he okay?" Zelda asks. She folds another hunk of bagel into her mouth. I zoom in on her face and she sticks her tongue out, giving me a full view of her chewed-up breakfast and her oversized tonsils.

"Zelda!" Dad barks. "Knock it off."

"Yes, he's okay...wherever he may be." Mom sighs. She fidgets with the zipper on her sweater.

"Well, that's good," Zelda tells her.

"What about that balloon order to the rest home?" I ask. "I bet it was fake."

"Jermaine, no camera allowed at the table, remember?" Dad warns. I did remember, but I was hoping he'd forgotten. I stand up from the table and back away, camera still running. This is important stuff.

"It's possible, Jermaine." Mom sips her coffee.

"You mean *probable*, not possible. The balloon order was obviously his excuse to get out of the house last night," Zelda says.

"Why would he want to do that?" I ask.

"We don't know any details, girls, really. We've told you all we know." That last line has a very detective-show feel to it. It sounds like something a perp might say to a police officer. *That's all I know.* (I learned the word *perp* on a reality crime show. It means "bad guy.")

"Jermaine, what are you doing?" My father sounds annoyed.

"You said not to film at the table. I'm not at the table." I see him look at my mom. They both shrug their shoulders and continue eating.

"Is he on vacation," I ask, "without Melinda and Aunt Edie?" I know from what I overheard that this is not the case. But I'm hoping to get a few more details that I might have missed while spying on my parents.

"We didn't say vacation," Dad explains. "We said… a…trip…" Dad looks at Mom for help.

"Did he run away?" I continue.

"No," Mom insists.

"Did he break the law?" Mom looks like she wants me to stop asking questions.

"Is he on the lam?" Zelda blurts.

"What do you mean *on the lamb?*" I ask.

"Oh girls," Mom interrupts, "I know it's strange, but I just can't tell you any more! Your uncle, for whatever reason, has decided to go away for a while. He did call to say he was fine, so we wouldn't worry." Mom shakes her head. "Aunt Edie hasn't told me any more—I don't think she knows any more than we do—so we all have to be patient. Even though it's very difficult," she adds angrily. Then she changes the subject. "I've got work to do for the Winter Pickle Palooza." She pushes her chair back from the table. "Who wants to help?"

Zelda shakes her head no. "Homework."

"Maybe later," I tell my mom. I don't have time for pickling right now.

Upstairs in my room I look up *lamb* in the dictionary. It says "young sheep." No surprise there, but it makes no sense. Then I find my Magic 8 Ball. I cradle it in my palms like a baby bird. I feel badly that my uncle is missing, especially bad for Melinda and Aunt Edie. But he's not *missing*, missing. It doesn't sound like he's in danger, thankfully. But the fact that no one knows where he is and why he left has added a whole new spin to my reality-TV show—a mystery. And Mom could be wrong. He could have done something bad, even if he didn't mean to. He might have broken a law by accident.

"Is Uncle Larry in danger?" I ask the Magic 8 Ball, tipping it upside down. The plastic triangle bobs side to side before it levels out.

"Definitely no," I read in the little window of the ball. I feel relieved.

"Did he do something bad?" I turn the ball around in my hands.

"My sources say no," it tells me.

"I knew he wouldn't have!" I say aloud. So there's really nothing for anyone to worry about. I will tell Aunt Edie and Melinda that everything will be okay. Maybe Uncle Larry has just been thinking about his pop-up-camper life again. Maybe he just needs a little vacation. Whatever the reason is for him not to have come home, Uncle Larry is going to be fine. Even though his leaving is still a big mystery, everything will be okay—it's all good, especially from a reality-show standpoint.

By dinner, Uncle Larry still hasn't come home. And he hasn't called again, either. Mom's been chomping at the bit to head over to Aunt Edie's. But Aunt Edie says if she comes over it might alarm Melinda that something is seriously wrong. And she's trying to remain calm about everything, at least until she hears from Uncle Larry again.

Downstairs in the basement we get ready for another family game night. Up until tonight, the Ping-Pong table has been used for sorting clean laundry and, of course, the underside has plenty of room for seven hamster cages. We bicker about who will partner with whom, so we do a round of rock, paper, scissors, and I win! I pick Dad to be my partner because I figure with all the arm exercise he gets from washing his car and sweeping out the garage he's probably the best player. It turns out we're all equally uncoordinated.

"Jermaine, if you put the camera down you could play more effectively," he tells me. Dad swats at the ball and misses. Mom swipes and misses, and I swear, if Zelda has to move any part of her body more than three inches, she doesn't. "Don't worry about serving inside the white line," Dad reminds Mom, "we're just playing for fun." Mom's serve bounces off the ceiling and lands in front of her. She tries again and gets it over the net. Dad stretches for the little white ball and misses by a long shot. Zelda renames the game "Ping-Pong for Ding-Dongs." We play for a few more painful minutes and I finally return a ball and get it over the net. The ball flies by Mom's shoulder and whacks the washing machine. Then Mom puts her paddle down on the table.

"I can't focus on Ping-Pong," she says. "I'm sorry, not with Larry gone and Edie a mess." Mom sighs. "Game night is canceled. I'm going to go check on Edie," she tells us, "whether she likes it or not."

"Can I come, too?" I ask. I reach for the edge of the

table for balance. Playing Ping-Pong with one eye looking through a lens has made me dizzy.

"Not tonight, Jermaine. I'm sure Edie doesn't want a crowd." Since when is two a crowd? Mom races up the stairs, skipping every other step. "I don't know when I'll be home. I'll call you," she tells us.

"Shouldn't we go look for him?" I ask Dad. "Should we put up posters?"

"He's not lost!" Zelda says. "Is he?" she asks.

"Well, he knows where he is, but no one else does," Dad says.

"Maybe he has amnesia and can't remember who he is," I say.

"That's not the case," Dad assures us, shaking his head. Then I realize something important: famous people can never go missing. I will never have to worry about getting lost and not being found. *There she is...Jermaine Davidson!* Wherever I go, someone will always recognize me, another excellent benefit of being famous. I turn my camera back on and zoom in on Susie, who has just snatched a hand towel from the laundry basket.

"Maybe Uncle Larry has a secret life," I suggest. I zoom in on Zelda.

"Maybe you should get a life." Zelda covers her face with her arm. The garage door goes up. I hear the rumble of Mom's pickup truck and the crunch of gravel under her tires. The door closes and she speeds away.

"There has to be a reason why he disappeared. Maybe we should get a search party together, or I could send some of my reality-show footage in to a news station. We were the last ones to see him before he went missing. I have it all on film. Maybe the police want to see it?" I say.

"Jermaine, he wasn't taken against his will," Dad

reminds me. "There's no need for search parties, police, or anything like that. I don't know why he left, or where to, but Uncle Larry left because he wanted to. He called Aunt Edie to explain that he was fine, remember?" Dad stacks the paddles together and puts them away.

I'm really glad that my Magic 8 Ball confirmed Uncle Larry is okay. But where he actually is and *why* he left is still a big mystery. My viewers will want to know more. People will start tuning out of my show if they're feeling frustrated. I kneel down under the Ping-Pong table and film each little hamster in its cage. Until I get the 411 on Uncle Larry, or at least a clue as to where he went, I'll have to distract my viewers with some extra exciting footage in the meantime. Because a good reality show can't leave the audience hanging in suspense forever. A famous reality-show producer doesn't leave unanswered questions or loose ends. The mystery of Uncle Larry will have to be solved. Maybe I can find him? I zoom in on Bernie, who is running on her squeaky wheel, faster and faster, but getting nowhere.

8
Panhandles

In Social Studies we are discussing the panhandle states. Lindsey Steinbrecker is asking why Mississippi doesn't qualify.

"It looks like it could have a panhandle with that boot heel," she argues.

"Boot heel?" Mrs. Finn asks.

"Yes, see that thing that looks like a boot heel that abuts the Gulf of Mexico?" She points to the wall-sized map that covers half the blackboard. *Who says "abut"?*

"A-*butt*?" Tyler Gibbs shouts out. The class laughs. Mrs. Finn twists her mouth into a crooked line. She stands at the front of the class, hands resting on the hips of one of those itchy-looking skirts she likes to wear.

"Stop that now," she scolds. "Lindsey makes a good point. It does look a bit like a panhandle."

Then my friend Ro passes me a note via Cameron Cane, who pokes me in the back with his pencil.

"Here," he says, handing me a small folded triangle.

The note says, *Let's hang out after school. Nina and I want you to film us. Bff Ro.*

K, I write on the same note and hold it under my chair for Cameron, who passes it back to Ro. Ever since I told my two best friends about my plan to be discovered by Rufus Carmichael and to get my family on national TV, they've been dying for a part in my show. I'm not allowed to bring my camera to school, which really stinks. The cafeteria lady, Miss Turnbull, is a screamer, and that would make for some nice footage.

I turn to a fresh page in my notebook and make a list of the reality shows on TV that I enjoy the most. I decide to organize my favorites into categories. There are some shows that feature people with talent, like the ones who can sing, or dance, or cook, or design and sew their own clothes. I really like those shows. Especially the ones where the audience gets to vote on who they think should win. I put at the top of that column the word *TALENT.* Then there are the shows like the nanny with the British accent who tries to get a bunch of bratty kids to behave, the married couples who trade families for a week, and the ridiculous women who all date the same man hoping to become his wife (weird, but so fun to watch!). These are the *NO TALENT* shows. I wonder where my show fits in. No one in my family can carry a tune. We stink at Ping-Pong. And the pillow I made in home ec looks like a trapezoid even though it's supposed to be a perfect square. We definitely don't fall under the *TALENT* category. We are even too plain for the *NO TALENT* column. What with my happily married parents, and Zelda and I being the furthest thing from brats, we are hopelessly ordinary. I tear the page out of my notebook and stuff it into my pocket.

"Jermaine." Mrs. Finn sounds irritated. "Are you paying attention?" she asks me. She stands in front of the map, wiping her glasses with the bottom of her blouse. She slides the funky blue frames back onto her face like she means business.

"Yes," I tell her.

"Then please answer the question." She waits. The room is quiet except for her booted foot tapping.

"Can you please repeat the question?" I ask. Mrs. Finn sighs.

"I asked if you could name three states that have panhandles." My eyes scan the map.

"Texas, Florida, and Oklahoma," I say with relief. I do know a panhandle when I see one.

"Very good, Jermaine," she says. "You're paying attention after all." Mrs. Finn spends the rest of the time in class discussing peninsulas and islands while I worry about my family's ordinariness. Finally, the bell rings and it's time for lunch.

The smell of meat loaf in the cafeteria makes me grateful for brown-bag lunches and peanut-butter sandwiches. Ro and I meet Nina and my cousin Melinda at our regular table next to the trash cans. There's still no news about my missing uncle. Mom told me at breakfast this morning that under no circumstances am I to ask Melinda any questions about what's going on. I sit next to my cousin.

"Any news about, you know..." I say quietly.

"What?" Ro asks. "What are you whispering about?"

"What news?" Nina asks. Nina dumps her lunch out of her bag. Her apple rolls across the table and I catch it before it falls off the edge.

"Nothing...," I say quickly, feeling sorry that I opened my big mouth. I roll the apple back to Nina. Melinda stares at me without saying a word.

"What? I heard you say 'news'!" Nina rips open a package of Pudding Cakes. Ro slurps her milk through a straw. Her dark eyes dart back and forth from me to Melinda, who is squinting at me.

"My dad is out of town, that's all, he'll be back soon," Melinda says calmly.

"What's the big deal if he's just out of town?" Ro asks. "My dad is out of town all the time. He flies to China like every other week practically."

"Oh, Jermaine is a big drama queen now that she's filming a reality show." Melinda glares at me. I shouldn't have said anything, but it just popped out, like a burp. *If I could just get one little clue that I could pass on to my audience...* Melinda kicks me under the table.

"You *are* a total drama queen," Ro announces. "When do we get to be in your show, anyway?"

"Have you heard back from Rufus Carmichael yet?" Nina asks.

"No, not yet, but it hasn't been very long. And I need you guys right away," I say. "There's no way I am going to be famous with my plain old ordinary family."

"Thanks," Melinda says sarcastically.

"Not you," I tell her. I take the crumpled reality-show list out of my pocket and smooth it out on the table. "Look. See this list? I'm trying to figure out what direction to take my show in." I point to the list of *TALENT* reality shows.

"Your mom's pickles are awesome!" Ro says. "She's talented."

I tell them about my plan to film Mom in the barn.

"But I can't have my show just be about her making pickles! A couple of cucumber-slicing scenes is plenty."

"Didn't your dad run the Boston Marathon?" Nina asks. "That's a talent."

"When he was in college," I tell her.

"Braids," Melinda says. She pulls the crust off her sandwich and presses it into a doughy lump. "Zelda braids."

"What are you talking about?" Ro asks.

"Zelda is an excellent braider." I say. "Maybe I can have a braiding competition."

I can tell no one really likes that idea.

"Who would she compete against?" Melinda asks.

"And who would really care?" Ro says.

"Some people might care," I say halfheartedly. "Then how about if Zelda braids your hair...it could be like a makeover show...new hairstyles."

"That would be fun," Ro says. "Is she really that good a braider?"

"She really is," I say. "She can do a bunch of different kinds."

"Like what?" Nina asks.

"Zelda invented names for each braid style, like the 'Low-slung.' Those are the braids that start low by your jaw," I explain. "They lie in front of your shoulders, like this..." I reach over and grab a handful of Ro's long hair and squeeze it together in my fist to make a ponytail. Then I lay it over the front of her shoulder to show her what I mean. "And 'Chopsticks,'" I continue. "Those are low-slung braids that stay straight and stiff behind your shoulders." I stand up and walk behind Ro. "'Handlebars' start high up on the head and come straight out to the sides." I demonstrate, again using Ro's hair. "And my favorite is the 'Drumstick,'" I say, taking my seat again.

"A single braid!" Nina guesses.

"Right!" I say.

"Drumstick? Like a chicken body part?" Ro asks.

"No, drumstick as in what you use to play the drums," I correct her.

"I don't like that name. It sounds like a chicken leg. You should change it," Nina says.

"How about PEG LEG!" Ro cackles.

"ELEPHANT TRUNK!" I yell.

"CAT TAIL!" Nina squeals.

"BROOM HANDLE!" Melinda shrieks.

"PAN HANDLE!" I shout.

"PIPE DOWN OVER THERE!" Miss Turnbull bellows.

"Tail*pipe!*" Melinda whispers. All of us howl with laughter. Miss Turnbull shuffles over to our table. I think she secretly wishes to be the school librarian, because she's always shushing everyone. Isn't a lunchroom supposed to be noisy? She could never work in a library anyway. Everyone knows she has the loudest voice in the school.

"DO I NEED TO SEND YOU GIRLS TO SEE THE PRINCIPAL?" she booms. The four of us freeze. The cafeteria is quiet. People snicker and stare. When I'm famous and Miss Turnbull sees my face on the cover of a magazine she'll tell all her friends, "*I know that girl, she's in my lunchroom!*" She'll wish she'd been nicer.

"That's better," she grumbles in her monster voice.

When I'm sure she's out of earshot I lean closer to the table and whisper: "My house. After school. Braids."

Rolling and...CUT!

9

It didn't take much to convince Zelda to participate in this makeover scene for my reality show—just my allowance for the next two months. But, I figure, soon I'll be rolling in dough; rich and famous go hand in hand.

Melinda, Nina, Ro, and I are crammed into the tiny upstairs bathroom Zelda and I share. Right after school, I set up a mini hair salon. A kitchen stool is at the counter in front of the mirror and Ro sits on top of it staring at herself. I've gathered every brush, comb, barrette, elastic, hair clip, and bottle of conditioner, styling gel and shampoo (even Mom's dandruff shampoo that makes her head smell like bug spray). It's all thrown together in the big white bucket Dad uses to clean the fish tank. Mom's pinking shears and a can of Scare-Hair left over from Halloween are next to each other by the sink.

"What do we need all this stuff for?" Ro asks. "I thought we were just doing braids."

"Aren't you all psyched to be on national TV?" I ask,

changing the subject. I'm really nervous about this scene for my reality show. Even though I told everyone we were just doing braids, I'm hoping they'll agree to be more adventurous.

Ro tips her head to the side and runs her fingers through her long, shiny hair. "Of course we are," she says. "Here." Ro takes her skull ring off her finger. "Wear this for extra luck. It will guarantee your show is a huge hit," she tells me.

"Thanks, Ro," I say. I slip the ring onto my index finger.

"You have to give it back after you get us on TV," she adds.

"I will," I assure her. Ro's skull ring really *is* lucky. It came out of the prize machine at her orthodontist's office. Ever since she's worn it, good things have happened—like finding two quarters on her bus seat the very next day, and her grandparents deciding to take her whole family to Disney World next week over February vacation. Ro sees the pinking shears and picks them up.

"What are these for?" she asks.

"Haircuts," I say nonchalantly. I pan my camera around the tiny bathroom.

Zelda pushes the bathroom door open. "Who's my first victim?" she asks, standing in the doorway.

Ro looks nervous. "Who said anything about haircuts?"

"I was thinking that braids are kind of boring," I say slowly. "This is a makeover segment for my reality show, remember? You know, a before-and-after thing?"

"Hey! I don't look like a *before*," Ro protests.

"I know that," I say quickly. "I meant *before* your new look and *after* your new look."

Zelda squeezes herself into the room. She picks up the can of Scare-Hair on the counter. "What's this?" she asks, putting it down. It tips over and rolls into the sink.

"In case someone wants highlights," I tell her. I point the camera first at Melinda's scalp, then at Ro's and Nina's.

"I like my hair color the way it is," Melinda says. "It's chestnut."

"I love your hair," I tell her. "It's just an option."

"I thought this was a braiding session," Ro repeats.

"I just told you—it's...whatever." I zoom in on her puzzled face. My stomach does a little flip. Maybe we *should* stick to braiding...even though it isn't very exciting reality-show stuff.

"By the way," Zelda says, "does anyone have dandruff? Or even worse, lice?" We all shake our heads no. "Good." Zelda digs through the bucket and pulls out a bottle of Bounce and Beautiful shampoo. "Let's go. Who's first?" she asks.

"Depends," Ro says slowly. "What are you going to do?"

"Over here by the tub," I instruct. "We have to wash your hair first." Ro slides off the stool. I film her kneeling on the floor.

"Lean your head forward," Zelda tells her. Ro crouches tightly up against the edge of the tub. Zelda turns the tap and guides Ro's head underneath it. Water runs over the back of Ro's neck and her shirt gets soaked.

"Watch it!" Ro yells. "That's freezing cold!"

"Whoops," Zelda says, adjusting the temperature and correcting her aim. She scrubs Ro's head, then rinses until the strands are squeaky clean and the bubbles disappear. Zelda twists her hair up in a towel. "Okay! Have a seat!" she orders. Melinda, Nina, and I fumble around trying to make room for Ro to get back to her seat at the mirror. Somebody steps on my foot and jostles the camera.

Ro's teeth are chattering when she gets back up on the

stool. "I'm soaked!" She shivers. Zelda pulls at Ro's tangled hair with a giant comb.

"Ow!" Ro cries. "You're ripping my hair out!"

"Sorry." Zelda struggles with the tangles.

"Be careful," I say. "Use cream rinse." While Zelda applies the cream rinse, I push pause on the camera, open a drawer under the counter, and pull out a magazine. "In *Teen* this month they have a big spread on funky haircuts and colors," I explain. "It's totally rock star! See,"—I hold it up—"it's zigzaggy...that's the new look, you know. Did you know that?"

"The new look, really?" Ro plucks the magazine out of my hand. "It's cute," she says. "But...I don't know...what if I hate it?"

"You don't have to go short, just a trim," I say. "Come on, this makeover scene will work really well for my show."

"Whoa! Am I supposed to use these?" Zelda holds up the jagged scissors.

"Hold on." Ro jumps off the seat. "Is this going to look good?"

"Are you kidding? You'll have a zigzag cut! Everyone at school will want one," I tell her. And I mean it. I imagine my friend's pretty face with an edgy new cut. I zoom in to get a close-up of Ro. "Once you're on national TV, you'll start a whole new trend. Maybe they'll call it the 'Ro Cut,'" I say excitedly. "It'll be great publicity for my show!" *A win-win for everyone!*

"You think so?" Ro smiles and sits back down.

"Can I have one, too?" Nina gushes.

"You do something different..." Ro says. "A Nina cut!"

"Are you all nuts?" Melinda asks. "No one is cutting my hair!"

"This is going to be so great!" I say.

"Do you know how to cut hair?" Ro asks Zelda.

"I learned how to use scissors in kindergarten, duh," Zelda tells her. Zelda holds the magazine and studies the page. "This is easy. I'll just cut straight across the ends." She walks around Ro, snipping at the bottom of her hair. "Can you all give me some elbow room?" Melinda steps back so she is pushed up against the bathroom wall, and I step inside the tub. "These scissors don't cut very well..." Zelda mumbles. "I think this side is a little uneven."

"Uneven?" Ro starts to fidget.

"Stop wiggling, please." Zelda continues to snip. "These things are really dull." I zoom out so I can get everyone in the scene.

"Stop cutting, it's too short!" Ro looks frantic. The right side of her hair is much shorter than the left side, and it curves in a shaggy arc above her shoulder.

"Okay, that's good, Zelda! That's ENOUGH!" I feel a huge wave of panic. It clogs my throat. Ro's hair is a disaster!

"It will look longer when it's dry," Zelda says nervously.

"Isn't it the other way around?" Nina asks. "Doesn't it get shorter when it's dry?" The room gets so quiet I can hear Melinda's watch ticking. Then Ro starts to say something but her voice is drowned out by the sound of the blow-dryer blasting. I keep filming because maybe when her hair is dry it *will* look better. Zelda shuts the dryer off. Ro's hair looks even worse.

"It's so frizzy." Ro's voice shakes. I feel sick to my stomach.

"Frizzy isn't so bad," Melinda and I say at exactly the same time.

Ro bursts into tears. This isn't what I had in mind. Ro

is supposed to have a new and improved look. I just put a terrible spin on the makeover segment…"Makeovers Gone Bad or Makeover Nightmares." Not a bad idea for a show, actually, if it wasn't featuring your best friend. *Should I keep filming?*

"No one cares about my hair!" she hiccups. Her face is red and puffy. Her nose is running. I turn my camera off and lay it on the counter.

"It's not so bad, it's…different," I say. I feel Nina jab me with her elbow as if to say *You-so-totally-know it's awful.*

"I saw you!" Ro shrieks at Nina. "I saw you poke her! I have eyes, you know, I can see…I see how awful I look!" Ro's crying gets louder.

"This was a stupid idea, Jermaine," my cousin tells me.

"I *know* that…" I pick up a brush. Frantically, I run it through what's left of Ro's hair. "Let me fix it," I say hopelessly. Nina tucks a piece of hair behind Ro's ear and Melinda tries to smooth out the frizz with the palms of her hands.

"Hold on. Everyone stop freaking out. Let me finish," Zelda says. "Step aside," she orders me. "The girl in the magazine has pink on the ends of her hair. Let me try something." She finds the can of hair color, shakes it, and squeezes a corroded-looking glob. Then she rubs and pats the color into the ends of Ro's chopped-up hair. It looks rusty and greasy. Ro starts to wail again. Big, loud, gut-wrenching sobs. "Well, *that* we can wash out," Zelda says softly.

"It's ugly!" Ro cries.

"We should have stuck to braids!" Nina says. She hands Ro some tissues.

"WHAT DID YOU DO TO ME?" Ro shrieks.

"The two of you wanted haircuts!" Zelda reminds Ro and Nina. "I tried to do a good job!" Zelda leaves the bathroom in a huff. When she slams the door a tuft of Ro's beautiful hair blows across my foot. Then Zelda opens the door again. "By the way, Jermaine...don't forget...for the next two months your allowance is mine..." She slams the door again.

Ro jumps off the stool. "Look at my hair! Look what Zelda did to my hair! And *you* let her do it!" she cries.

"It wasn't supposed to...be...like...that..." I stumble over my words.

"Well, you can't put this in your show," she says.

A good *friend* wouldn't put this scene in her show. But...a good *producer* would. "But...it's reality TV..." I say.

"Jermaine!" Nina yells.

"Are you joking?" Ro is furious. I'd be mad, too, if someone chopped my hair off. "All this reality-TV stuff has affected your brain!" she continues. "You don't care about anything anymore except getting famous!"

"I do care!" I say. A heavy load of fear creeps around my heart when I wonder if she's right.

"No you don't! I'm the one with ruined hair, not you!"

I pick up the jagged scissors and cut off a hunk of my own hair. I reach around my head, snipping away. Then I switch to the other side. I manage to do just as bad a job as Zelda.

"Are you serious?" Melinda asks me.

Ro and I stand side by side looking into the mirror. It is hard to tell who looks worse.

"There. Now you're not the only one with an awful haircut." I smile at her. I think I see a tiny smile back. Maybe I can be a good friend and a good producer at the same time.

I help Ro rinse the awful canned color out of her hair. An orange river of Scare-Hair runs along the bottom of the tub. It flows gently toward the rim of the drain until, with a loud sucking noise, the water is pulled into an angry spin. I watch it disappear.

10

Are You There, Mr. Carmichael?

Dear Mr. Carmichael,

Talk about drama! My sister, Zelda, made a mess of my best friend's hair with my mom's zigzag scissors and I got it on film. Have you ever done anything like that for one of your own shows? My plan was to give her a makeover but things got out of hand. My sister turned out to be a lousy hairdresser. I felt so bad for my friend that I cut my hair off, too. The upside of all this is that I did get some really great footage for my show (though my friend doesn't want it in the show!) What would you do? Even worse than that (besides our awful haircuts) is that when Mom saw what Zelda did to Ro's hair and what I did to mine, she was really mad. We can't watch TV or use the computer (except for homework). And my mom took away my camera for a solid week! It's not that we didn't deserve to be punished (because we did) but it's totally unfair that I got three punishments (TV, computer, and camera) and Zelda only got two (TV and computer). Then to top it all off, Ro's mom wasn't happy, either. She took Ro to the hairdresser to "fix" the cut Zelda gave her and Zelda and I have to pay for it. Mom's taking it out of our allowances. That's a whole other problem for me, but I won't bother you with details. Filming is on hold for the rest of the week. I'll keep you posted.

It sure would be great to hear back from you really soon. Especially now that my show is on hiatus and I have plenty of time to read through my mail . . . not that I ever get any . . . hint, hint.

Your patient fan,
Jermaine

PS Did you like my idea about The Country Life? *You should come to the Pickle Palooza. It's in a couple weeks and the whole town will probably be there . . . including yours truly!*

11
Good Things

"I like your new haircut," I tell Ro when I plop down next to her on the bus. We both had to have our hair cut yesterday by a real hairdresser after the "makeover." It's just below her chin. Ro doesn't say thanks or anything. She gets up out of the seat and squeezes past me.

"Sit down!" the bus driver calls out when he sees her. I look up to see the driver's nervous eyeballs in the rearview mirror. "We're moving," he warns.

I twist around in my seat and try to make eye contact with Ro, but she pretends she doesn't see me. "RO!" I shout. "I thought you weren't mad at me?" She sits three rows behind me with a kid she hardly knows.

"Yup, she's mad at you. She's not talking," Lindsey Steinbrecker, who's sitting behind me, comments. "What did you do to tick her off?" she asks. I ignore her. "Does it have something to do with your twin haircuts?"

"Stop it," I tell her. Ro doesn't understand what it takes to be a famous person. It's hard work. It involves sacrifice. I rub my thumb over the lucky skull ring. I hope she doesn't ask for it back.

Ro ignores me all day even though I've said I'm sorry like a hundred times. Melinda and Nina can't convince her to forgive me. She won't come to the phone when I call her after school, either.

"I'm sorry, honey, she's still upset about the whole hair thing," her mother says. Gosh, even her mom isn't angry anymore. She called me honey. "I'll try to talk to her," her mom tells me before I hang up.

My Magic 8 Ball doesn't give me a straight answer when I ask if Ro and I will ever be friends again. *"Ask again later"* and *"Can't tell you now"* keep bobbing in the window.

Ro stays mad at me for most of the week. By Thursday, she still isn't speaking to me. And then after school, something *really* unsettling happens. Nina, her mom, and I visit Granny Viola at the Bluebird Nest & Rest Senior Home and Granny V keeps forgetting who I am.

"Look who's here," Pat tells Granny V She puts her arm around Granny Viola's tiny, round shoulders. "You've got some company." Granny Viola sits at a table with a blanket over her lap. She cuts coupons from a stack of newspapers.

"Hi, Mrs. Church." I hand her a small loaf of banana bread Mom and I baked the night before.

"Who are you?" she says in a whispery voice. "Who's that?" she asks Nina's mother, pointing at *me* with a knobby finger.

"You know Jermaine, Mother, she's been here many times," Nina's mom reminds her.

"Yes, that's right." Granny squints at me. "I forget sometimes," she says in her quiet voice. And she isn't kidding. Ten minutes later she asks again who I am! Not a good sign for someone whose main goal in life is to become famous.

My luck changes on Friday. The skull ring finally kicks into gear. Besides it being the last day before February vacation (yay!), I convince Mom to let me have my camera back. All week I have been extremely persistent. One thing I've learned since becoming a reality-show producer is that persistence does pay off. Ask any famous person, and they'll tell you the same thing. I've heard them say so in interviews on TV.

"The scales of justice are *not* balanced," I kept telling Mom, referring to the fact that my punishment was harsher than Zelda's. I got that line from one of those courtroom reality shows. At the beginning of the show, a serious voice announces, *"In Judge Wanda's courtroom, the scales of justice are BALANCED!"* And then some aggressive music plays, with lots of violins and cymbals crashing, and Judge Wanda enters the courtroom in her long black robe holding her little wooden hammer. After hearing me quote that "scales of justice are not balanced" line about twenty times, Mom finally broke down and said, "Oh for Pete's sake, use your flippin' camera already!"

Then at school another good thing happens. Ro forgives me! First, I catch her staring at me a few times. Then in art, I pick up her pastel when it falls to the floor, and she thanks me! By lunchtime, she's back at our regular table. Ro bites her sandwich and hands me an Oreo—a peace offering.

"I'm not mad anymore," she says.

"Good," I say. "And I really do like your new haircut." Ro starts to giggle. "What?" I ask. Melinda and Nina look at Ro, too. "What's so funny?" I ask again. I scrape the white cream inside the cookie with my top teeth.

"The whole makeover thing, if you think about it," she says. "I can't believe I was stupid enough to trust Zelda to cut my hair!"

"I'm glad I didn't let her touch my hair," Nina says.

"Yes, especially after she butchered Ro!" Melinda interrupts. Melinda, Nina, and I crack up.

"It's not *that* funny," Ro says seriously.

"No it's not," I say quickly. We quit laughing.

"Thanks for cutting your hair off, Jermaine," Ro tells me.

"I like having matching cuts!" I smile, though my hair is so frizzy it looks more like an Afro compared to Ro's silky bob. "Thanks for letting Zelda cut your hair," I say.

"I'm glad you're not using that makeover disaster in your show," she says. "I'd be so embarrassed. My nose was running, too."

Thinking about what to do with that scene makes me lose my appetite. I push my sandwich aside. What would Rufus Carmichael do? If Ro was his best friend he would probably take it out. But he already has so many successful shows! I don't have any!

"I still want to be in your show, though," Ro continues. "Maybe when I get back from Florida you can film me when I'm tan, okay?" She smiles at me and tries to flip her hair, but it's too short.

"Sure." I tell her. "Don't worry. You'll all be in it...even if it's just a cameo..."

"What does that mean?" Nina asks. But I don't answer because I'm distracted by what I just said! *Even if it's just a cameo*...it's like Hollywood jargon. I feel a twinge of famous-ness wash over me, which makes me feel a whole lot better.

After lunch, yet another good thing happens. Let me remind you that without TV and computer all week, and without my camera until this morning, I have had a lot of time to think about what to do next with my reality show. All this talk about hair has given me a great idea.

Last month over the Martin Luther King holiday, the roof leaked and our class pet Sugarplum, a really friendly guinea pig, got drenched, and cold, and died. Besides being tragic and sad, the room stank really badly when we got back from the long weekend. We had to keep the windows open, even though it was like eighteen degrees outside. (This is obviously not the good thing I was referring to.) So, I suggest to Mrs. Finn that it would be wise to have someone bring our new class pet home over the February vacation week.

"What if the roof leaks again?" I ask her. "Or there's some other disaster?"

"That's a great idea, Jermaine," Mrs. Finn agrees. "Let's draw numbers to see who gets to take Harry home for the week."

"Draw numbers?" I ask. "But it's my idea," I remind Mrs. Finn.

"Yes, it's a very prudent idea," she tells me. "Who knows what I mean by *prudent*?" she asks the rest of the class. Lindsey volunteers to look it up, of course, even though most everyone figures it out by context.

"Smart," someone says.

"Good," someone else suggests. While everyone tries one-upping each other's definitions, I'm thinking that the idea I have for getting some amazing footage for my reality show cannot happen without the class pet.

"Mrs. Finn," I say to my teacher, "I really need to take Harry home for the week."

"I want to take Harry home! Let me take Harry." Tyler Gibbs sticks his head in front of Mrs. Finn's face, blocking me from her view.

"Excuse me. I was talking to Mrs. Finn." I step around Tyler so Mrs. Finn sees me.

"Please, please, I'll take good care of him," he pleads.

"But it was my idea," I remind Mrs. Finn again. "I'll do a really good job." Mrs. Finn pushes at her bottom lip with a boney finger. *Persistence, persistence, persistence*, I chant inside my head. "Please," I say again.

"Somebody's pushy," Tyler says to me.

"Enough!" Mrs. Finn tells us. (Here comes the good part...) "Hmmmm..." she says. "You really want the job as pet-sitter, don't you?" she asks me.

"So do I," Tyler pleads.

"Jermaine did ask first. It *was* her idea. Yes, I do think that's fair," she tells me, nodding. She turns to Tyler. "You can take Harry home over *spring* break," she says to him.

"YES!" I shout. "Thanks, Mrs. Finn!" Tyler slumps his shoulders in defeat.

"Hey," I say, "you can come and visit him if you want to."

"Thanks. But it's not the same."

"Ewwwww! Why in the world would you want to take that creepy thing home? I wouldn't be able to sleep at night knowing he could escape," Ro shivers.

"Harry is not creepy," I say. "He's cute." So cute, as a matter of fact, he'll be guest starring in my reality show, wink, wink.

12
Ping

Since Mom is petrified of spiders, I figure it would be to everyone's advantage (especially mine) if I didn't go into too much detail about our new class pet. Standing in the doorway of the pickle barn, I hold the cage behind my left leg. Mom barely looks up from her pot of brine when I tell her I'll be taking care of Harry for the week.

"Just keep him in the basement with the rest of the rodents," she says.

The next morning when I come down for breakfast, Mom is spooning something red and relish-y into a tiny paper cup.

"Try some of this," she says to me, smiling into the camera. Her hair is still tucked into a net that she must have forgotten to take off when she came in from the barn. "I need a new product for the Pickle Palooza. This is pickled red pepper relish," she tells me. I zoom in on the open jar and get a close-up of a chopped onion.

"Is it spicy?" I ask. I pick up one of the tiny white

spoons, the same kind the ice-cream scooper-person uses when you want to try a flavor you're unsure of.

"No, the peppers are sweet," she explains, "but the pickles make it tangy." I put the relish in my mouth and let it sit on my tongue for a second before I swallow.

"It's really good," I tell her.

"You like it?" She smiles. "Do you think the judges will give it first prize?"

"Definitely!" I tell her. The Palooza is the most important event of the year for a small pickle business like Mom's. Winning the Best New Pickle Product prize would be really special—especially since the Palooza is being held in Bangor this year.

Dad comes into the kitchen and kisses the top of my head. He kisses Mom right on the lips.

"Hellllllooooo..." I say. "This is a family show!" I press the pause button. Mom and Dad laugh.

"It's just a good-morning kiss, don't be so silly," she tells me. "Try this." She hands Dad a bit of the relish. "This is a winner, I know it," she says excitedly.

"Mmmmm...a winner..." Dad nods his head.

"I've still got lots of work," Mom chatters. "I want to make sure I've got extra jars of everything...enough to sell, and for sampling of course"—Mom turns the lid back onto the jar of relish—"and I want to take Edie out today...help take her mind off...things." I turn the camera back on.

"When is Uncle Larry coming back?" I ask.

"Not sure," Mom says quietly. Then she exhales loudly, shaking her head.

"He will come back, right?" Mom and Dad look at each other and then at me.

Dad puts his hand on my shoulder. "I know, honey, it's a difficult situation, isn't it?" he says.

"And it's...weird..." I say. "When are you coming back from lunch?" I ask my mother.

"I'm not sure exactly," she says.

I can tell by the look Mom gives Dad that she thinks I'm worried that she won't come back, like Uncle Larry. But I'm not worried about that. I know my mom would never take off. She would never do that to us. I miss my uncle but I am angry at him, too. How could he do this to Aunt Edie and Melinda? What was he thinking, running away from his family? And he sure isn't making my life any easier, keeping my reality-show audience dangling.

Mom slides her hand down the side of my cheek and under my chin. "I'll be home by four o'clock, okay?" I nod.

While Mom is with Aunt Edie, Melinda spends the day with us. Here's what I get on film: Melinda and I run errands with Dad at Walmart. While Dad looks for drawer organizers for the messy drawers he's always complaining about, Melinda and I make our way over to the small-animal-supply aisle. I film Melinda sliding seven honey sticks off the steel pole and tossing them into the red shopping basket. Melinda is in love with the idea of being on TV.

"Stop smiling into the camera," I direct her. "Act natural."

"Oh, sorry, like this?" She turns away from me and pretends I'm not there.

"That's better. Turn sideways now so I can get your face. Grab some bedding for the hamsters," I tell her. Melinda takes a big block of bedding off the shelf. It doesn't fit in the little basket so she grasps it by the plastic handle that's attached to the packaging. She holds it up for the camera and turns her mouth up in a ridiculously fake smile.

"This isn't a commercial. Just pretend the camera's

not here," I instruct. Then we meet Dad at the checkout counter as planned, and he buys us a roll of Life Savers Gummies on the way out, nothing too exciting.

We stop at the dry cleaners. Through the back window of the car, I film Dad when he slams the trunk on the long plastic sheets protecting the clothes. He opens the trunk back up and tucks the plastic inside. We pull up to the drive-thru window at the bank, and the teller waves into the camera. I film Dad pumping gas. Then I zoom in on him squeegeeing the windshield clean. Dad takes us to China Sail for lunch and we eat kung pao chicken. Melinda tries to use chopsticks but makes a mess and drops a peanut in her lap. We bring the leftovers home in a little white box for Zelda and her friend Katrina. It's all so utterly ordinary. When I am famous, I will hire someone to do all my boring errands, and a personal chef to make kung pao chicken every night of the week, if I feel like it.

At three thirty, Mom calls and says she'll be home in half an hour. Time to clean the hamster cages! Zelda and Katrina come downstairs to help. Katrina has never cleaned a hamster cage, never mind seven, and is pretty excited.

"Don't you have seven hamsters, not eight?" Katrina peeks under the Ping-Pong table.

"Oh, that's the guinea pig from my sister's classroom. She's pet-sitting," Zelda tells her.

"There's a guinea pig in that small cage?" Katrina asks.

"Harry's not a guinea pig!" Melinda laughs. Zelda screams when she peeks inside Harry's cage.

"What the heck—wh-wh-where did this thing come from?" she stutters.

"What is it?" Katrina bends down to see. "EEW!"

"I told you, our guinea pig died," I remind Zelda.

"You didn't say they replaced it with a disgusting spider," Zelda says.

"You didn't ask," I tell her. I look up at the clock. "But don't worry. He's very sweet."

"SWEET? Mom is going to flip when she finds out. He won't be staying here tonight."

"I plan to drop him off at Tyler's later. I only need him for a segment for my show," I explain.

"Obviously at Mom's expense," Zelda says angrily.

I wish she hadn't said that. I'm already feeling a little uncomfortable with this plan in the first place. "Zelda, just clean the cages so I can film, already," I tell her. I zoom in on Harry's cage. He's tucked away under his spiral of bark. "Wave hi, Harry!" I say, trying to lighten the moment.

Zelda places each hamster inside a plastic ball to keep them from running away while we change the soiled bedding. In a few minutes, seven colorful "run around" balls roll across the basement floor.

"Don't they get claustrophobic in those things?" Katrina asks.

"Claustrophobic? They live in a cage." Zelda laughs. "They're out of luck if they're claustrophobic."

Soon I hear the garage door.

"Quick! Mom's home! Someone let Harry out of his cage!" I order.

"Why?" Zelda practically squawks.

"Where is everyone?" Mom asks loudly.

"Just do it! Hurry up!"

"This is mean!" Melinda tells me.

"I know, but it's only mean for a second while I get some footage for my show!"

"Is he poisonous?" Katrina asks.

"Yes," Zelda tells her, "you might die if he bites you." Katrina freezes.

"No," I say, "that's not true." I hear Mom talking to Dad in the kitchen and I'm worried I am going to miss my chance for some excellent footage. "Come on! Someone let him out. It's only for a few seconds and I'll put him back in."

"I can't," Melinda says. "I don't want to." She re-hangs the water bottles onto their metal hooks.

"Hold this," I say to Katrina, shoving my camera into her hands. Katrina holds the camera up to her eye and films Zelda pouring seed into the hamsters' dishes. I scoot under the Ping-Pong table and pull the top off Harry's cage.

"Jermaine! Do not take that thing out!" Zelda looks scared.

"It's okay, Zelda. I know what I'm doing. Come on, Harry." I tip the bark back and scoop him into my hand. "ARRRHGGG!" I scream, and drop him to the floor. I'm such a wimp. Luckily he isn't injured.

"She would have been plenty scared just seeing him in his cage!" Zelda says.

I hadn't thought of that. I guess I could have filmed her discovering him in his cage. It still would have been dramatic...but now it's too late. I hear Mom's footsteps on the creaky basement stairs. I grab the camera back from Katrina. Zelda screams.

"What's happening, girls?" Mom sings out to us. "What's all the screaming about?" She's carrying a basket of dirty laundry.

All of a sudden I feel an overwhelming urge to warn her.

"Don't come down here!" I shout.

"Hey," Mom manages to say just as she reaches the bottom of the staircase. One of the hamsters jogging inside a green ball spins toward Harry. Mom sees the tarantula right away. She drops the basket and screams just as the ball smacks into Harry's fuzzy legs. Harry makes a mad scurry out of harm's way. Mom's manic screaming somehow pushes the *guilt-ridden* Jermaine aside while the *producer* Jermaine takes over. I film her jumping up and down.

"Uh-oh," I hear Katrina say behind me.

"Put that thing in his cage!" Zelda squeals. Mom flaps her arms so frantically it looks like she could fly around the room. (That would really be something!) She lets loose a few choice words which I'll have to bleep out since they could qualify my very own show as one I'm not allowed to watch! Mom continues to shriek and...oops! I didn't realize she knew so many swear words!

"Where the BLEEEEEEEEEEEEEEP did that horrible thing come from? Why? WHY is it in my house?"

"It's the class pet," I say sheepishly.

"What class pet? *WHOSE* CLASS PET? GUINEA PIG..." Mom's words are all jumbled. I zoom in on her face. She actually looks ill. That's when *guilt-ridden* Jermaine kicks *producer* Jermaine right in the gut. I shut the camera off.

"WHERE IS IT? WHERE'D IT GO?" she cries. I look around the basement floor. Harry has disappeared. "I CAN'T STAY HERE!" she shrieks. "I can't stay in this house with that thing on the loose. I can't...I can't...," she pants. Her pink slipper flies off as she runs up the steps. "CLAAARRRRRK!"

"It won't hurt you, Mom, I promise!" I call after her.

"Uh-oh," Katrina says again.

I hear Mom's frantic voice through the ceiling. I feel bad that she's so upset, but at the same time I feel a ping of excitement—a tiny jolt that sends a chill straight through me. Then I hear the sound of Mom's truck backing out of the driveway. I rush up the stairs to the kitchen.

"Wait! Mom! I'm sorry!" I shout. But I'm too late. She's gone. And the ping of excitement is quickly forgotten.

13
Losers Weepers

"I am so angry with you, Jermaine," Mom shouts in my ear. It is less than ten minutes after Mom peeled out of the driveway that she calls me from Aunt Edie's. "How could you do this to me?"

"I'm sorry," I tell her. "I'm really, really sorry." That last *sorry* barely makes it out of my throat, it's so tight with shame.

"How could you bring that thing into our home when you know how I hate spiders? You know how I hate them, Jermaine! Ugh! I feel like something's crawling over me!"

Before I have a chance to respond, Mom says: "I'm staying at Aunt Edie's until you find that monster. I can't imagine having that thing show up in my bed! You're in big trouble, Jermaine! *Big* trouble!" she tells me.

"I'm sure it won't go all the way upstairs to your bed, Mom," I say hopefully, scanning the kitchen and then the staircase that leads to the bedrooms.

"You don't know that, Jermaine! You *do not* know

that! And I am not going to find out if it can or it can't! Find that horrible thing, and get it out of the house, because I am not coming home until you do!"

"But what if..." I start to say. *What if I never find it?* Panic rattles through me when the thought crosses my mind.

"And tell your father to pack me a bag with my toothbrush and underwear...tell him to check the suitcase first, just in case...oh never mind! The spider could be setting up a nest in one of those suitcases right now! Who knows where that thing could be...it could be in my underwear drawer...oh no, it won't lay eggs, will it? Oh please, Jermaine! Tell me it won't lay eggs!"

That never occurred to me. Harry is a boy, but then again we have a hamster named Bernie with seven kids.

All I can think of to say is, "I don't think spiders make nests."

"Jermaine, get off the phone and help us find this spider!" Dad yells up from the basement.

"I'll find him. Don't worry," I tell her.

"PLEASE, Jermaine. You find him, and then you find someone else to spider-sit, because your pet-sitting days are over! Do you understand?"

"Yes...I promise...I have to go, Mom," I say. "Bye." When I hang up, I realize that I have a missing Uncle *and* a missing spider and now *Mom* is gone, too.

Down in the basement Susie follows Dad around. Dad looks under the dryer, Susie looks under the dryer. Dad looks behind the sink, Susie looks behind the sink.

"We're probably going to have to move," Zelda says.

"Stop standing around and wasting time," Dad commands. "It has to be around here somewhere." I check under the Ping-Pong table. The hamsters are back in their cages. Susie comes over and sniffs at the floor.

After an hour or so of searching, we still haven't found Harry. "Maybe he's gone upstairs," Dad says, looking up at the ceiling. There are pipes and wires and all sorts of great hiding places up there. Maybe there's a crack big enough for a tarantula to squeeze through. Maybe he took the stairs.

"Nice going," Zelda frowns. "You scared your own mother out of the house."

"She'll be back once we find Harry," I say.

"*If* we find Harry." Zelda looks around. "Do you see a creepy tarantula anywhere? We may never, ever find it...all because you're so obsessed with being famous." She scowls at me. "Parents don't run out on their family for nothing!" I can tell by the look of horror on Zelda's face she's sorry she said that the minute it flies out of her mouth. Melinda, who is quietly looking between some half-empty paint cans, bursts into tears. I cover my mouth in surprise. Katrina looks completely confused.

"It's one big disaster around here after another!" my father says sharply. He walks over to Melinda and puts his arms around her. "It's okay, sweetheart," he tells her softly.

Zelda walks over and hugs Melinda, too. "Sorry, Mel, I didn't mean to say that, I...I'm sorry." I don't know what to say. I wonder why a father *would* run away from his family. It has to be pretty bad—much worse than a runaway tarantula. I wish I had magic powers to bring Uncle Larry home. I wish the roof hadn't leaked in Mrs. Finn's classroom. I wish Harry was Sugarplum the guinea pig or that I had let Tyler Gibbs take Harry home when he begged me to. I wish Mom hadn't left because of me and that Zelda hadn't said what she said. Maybe I should forget all about this reality show. What's so great about being a producer, anyways? I use my camera to zoom in on the maze of wires and pipes above me. Harry has to be here somewhere. I scan the back corners of the basement. Through the lens, I see Melinda's sobbing has stopped. She sniffs and hiccups.

I shut the camera off and walk over to her. "Are you all right?" She nods. I give her a hug. "Everything is going to be okay," I tell her, though I'm not so sure about that.

"Jermaine," Dad says firmly. "Hand over that camera right now!"

"But it's turned off! I'm looking for Harry," I say quickly. All those wishes I tucked away a few minutes ago spill out inside my head. They seem to be fighting with the horrific thought of losing my camera again...which reminds me *exactly* what's so great about being a producer...being famous.

"There will be no camera until you find that spider!" Dad takes it out of my hand.

"Please, Dad," I beg, "I just got it back yesterday!"

The phone rings. Dad looks toward the staircase. "I'll be right back." He lays the camera on the Ping-Pong table before he runs upstairs to answer it. "Keep looking," he tells us.

"I think I see him," Zelda shouts. She's peering into the small space between the washer and dryer. "Quick! Get me a broom!" Katrina finds a mop in the corner of the basement. She hands it to Zelda, who flips the handle to the floor and squeezes it into the small space.

"Don't hurt him," I warn. "Mrs. Finn will never trust me again."

"She shouldn't have trusted you in the first place," Zelda says. I hear Dad's muffled voice upstairs. I pick up the camera. Since we may have found the spider, then technically it's okay to use it. I focus on Zelda and then where the mop handle disappears into the tight space.

"Come on, Harry, I see you." Zelda jabs with the mop. "I'll slide him out, but I'm not touching him," she says.

"Just be careful," I remind her. Zelda drags the handle out.

"Got him!" she yells. I zoom in on the basement floor. It's only a balled-up black sock. "Oops, guess not." Zelda pushes the sock back between the washer and dryer. "Well, it looked like a spider," she says. I quickly turn the camera off and place it back on the table.

"I think we need to split up," I say anxiously. What if Harry is lost forever? That would be a complete disaster. We'll have to sell this house and buy a new one. Where will Mom make her pickles? What if she has to shut down her business? I know one thing for sure. She'll never live in a house with a tarantula on the loose. And I'll never get my camera back. I'll never be famous! The thought of riding the bus to school instead of taking a limo is depressing.

"Zelda, you and Katrina stay down here. Melinda, you take the first floor, and I'll search the bedrooms," I instruct.

"I don't think he's upstairs," Zelda says. "Splitting up would be a waste of time."

"He's not down here," Melinda says. "I'll go upstairs and look."

"It's a waste of time!" Zelda insists. We argue back and forth. None of us notices Dad coming back downstairs until we hear him clear his throat. We look up. He's smiling.

"You found Harry!" I shout. Dad doesn't answer me. Instead, he puts his hand on Melinda's shoulder and hands her the phone.

"Your father would like to speak to you," he says.

14
Finders Creepers

Melinda's face turns whiter than its usual white. Slowly she takes the phone from Dad's hand and holds it to her ear.

"Hello..." she barely whispers. We stand in a half circle around her, gawking inappropriately, Dad, too. Finally Dad comes to his senses and hustles us upstairs.

"What happened?" Zelda asks frantically. "Where is he, is he home?"

"Where is he?" I repeat. "What happened?" Katrina's head turns from side to side like she's watching a tennis match.

"Hang on," Dad says. "Stay here." He runs back down the basement stairs.

"Wait!" I shout.

"Stay up there," Dad orders. Zelda and I start to sneak down the stairs, but the steps are too creaky. We stand still. We can hear Melinda.

"What's going on?" Katrina whispers. Zelda starts to explain.

"Shush! I can't hear," I tell them.

"Okay, Daddy," she's saying. "I miss you, too. I love you, too." She starts to cry. My father must take the phone at this point, because I hear him say, "Yes, okay, that's good, Larry."

"Should we go downstairs now?" I whisper to Zelda.

"Yes, go." She pokes me with her fingers.

We clomp down the basement stairs. Dad has finished speaking. The phone is on the Ping-Pong table next to my forbidden camera. Zelda and I don't say a word. Melinda is smiling, but wiping away tears. This surprises me and makes me wonder how it's possible to smile and cry at the same time...like when it's raining but the sun is shining...weird.

"Is Uncle Larry okay?" Zelda asks.

"Yes," says my father. Then he asks Melinda, "Are you okay?" Melinda nods her head.

"Where is he?" I ask.

"He didn't say." Then Dad gives us a look that says, *Not now!*

"Can I call my mom?" Melinda interupts.

"Of course." Dad hands her the phone. Then Dad turns to us and says, "Let's check upstairs for the spider."

Once upstairs I ask, "What's the matter with Uncle Larry?" Dad drags his hand over the top of his hair.

"It seems Uncle Larry is alive and well," he tells us.

"We know that already," I say impatiently.

"Did he do something bad? Is that why he hasn't come home?" Zelda asks. I imagine filming poor Uncle Larry's arrest, handcuffed and led to a police car. The cop places his hand on Uncle Larry's head to protect it from getting bumped. Then the officer guides Uncle Larry, butt-first and bent at the waist, into the backseat of the police cruiser. Blue lights are flashing. It's probably like a scene from *Cops and Convicts*, one of the reality shows my parents won't let me watch.

"Look, we've been through all this and there's not much to tell," Dad explains.

"Come on, he must have said something," I prod.

"He said he had to work something out." Dad stops talking when Melinda walks into the room. I so wish I had my camera to record the awkward moment of silence. Then Dad says: "I'm going to pick up some pizza in a while and we'll all have dinner with Mom and Aunt Edie. But first we must find that spider!" *That's it?* The missing uncle calls and all I get is…pizza? And what exactly does Uncle Larry have to work out? There has to be a reason he took off. Even Harry has a reason…he probably *is* claustrophobic and likes it out of his cage. Or he's confused and doesn't know how to get back. Maybe Uncle Larry feels claustrophobic…but that doesn't make sense…he loved living in that cramped camper all those years. Maybe he's confused…I'm confused right now, but I wouldn't run away.

Zelda and Katrina help Dad search the kitchen and family room, while Melinda and I decide to search the bedrooms. Melinda heads to my parents' bedroom, and I check my own room. Zelda won't let me in hers, even to rescue a tarantula. But Harry's nowhere to be found.

I sit on my bed and think. I twirl the skull ring around my finger a few times. I need some good luck and some answers. Inside my desk drawer I find my Magic 8 Ball wedged between a stash of magazines and my jewelry box. I hold the 8 ball in both hands and slide myself to the floor, leaning my back against the side of my bed. Before I get to the important questions I test its accuracy.

"Do I have blue eyes?" I ask. I gently tip the ball back and forth. I peer into the foggy window.

"*Yes—definitely,*" it says. It's dead on.

"Will Uncle Larry come home soon?"

"*Signs point to yes*" is the answer.

"Will I find Harry?"

"*Without a doubt,*" it assures me. I am feeling much better now. Finding Harry solves the rest of my problems. Mom will come home and I'll get my camera back! But I have one more thing I need to know.

"Will I be famous?" I close my eyes and turn the ball around in my hands.

"*Ask again later,*" it says. How much later, I wonder? I wait a few seconds.

"Will I be famous?" I ask again.

"*Better not tell you now,*" it says.

"Why?" I shout at it. I ask a third time but reword the question in case it didn't understand me the first two times.

"*Famous...*is that how people will describe me?" This time I shake the ball for several seconds.

"*Don't count on it*" floats into the window.

"What? You don't know what you're talking about!" I yell at the ball. But it dawns on me that if the ball is wrong about me being famous, then maybe it's wrong about everything else, too! Maybe Uncle Larry isn't coming home! Maybe Harry is lost forever! I'll never get my camera back! And what about my mother...she has to come home eventually! Doesn't she? I want to ask the ball. Instead I throw it roughly to the floor.

"You don't even know what a tarantula is!" I yell as it rolls under my dresser. *Of course I'll be famous! What does a stupid plastic ball know, anyway?*

Susie comes into my room wagging her tail. She lowers her head and nudges my shoulder. I scratch behind one of her ears. She whines and drops something beside me on the floor. "Sorry, Susie, I can't play right now." I reach between her paws for the furry toy. Before I have the chance to chuck it out my bedroom door, it moves in my hand. Susie tries to snatch it back, but before she can, I stand quickly. I lift Harry, safe in my palm, up and out of harm's way.

15
Aunt Edie

On the way to Aunt Edie's, we drop Harry off at Tyler Gibbs's house. That is where he will spend the rest of his February vacation. Thankfully, Tyler's mom isn't completely freaked out by Harry. Not that she's a big fan of tarantulas, as she told us when we called. But she agreed to take Harry in.

"Really, she moved out?" Mrs. Gibbs asks. It sounds ridiculous when you actually hear someone say it out loud. Dad and I stand on the front porch of their house. Dad shoves his hands into his pant pockets and hunches up his shoulders. I can tell he's embarrassed.

"Well, not really *moved out*, moved out." He chuckles to make it all sound like a funny thing. He bobs his head like a weirdo. "Go figure!" he says in a voice too loud. "Well, here he is. Enjoy!" Dad smiles at me and I pass the cage to Tyler, who can't take Harry out of my hands fast enough.

"I should have taken him home in the first place," he tells me.

"That probably would have been best," Dad agrees, head still bobbing. I say nothing.

After we leave, we drop Katrina off at her house, pick up pizza, and head over to Aunt Edie's. I haven't been over since Uncle Larry disappeared. I have my camera back. Thank heavens for Susie! I'm going to see to it that she gets a steak for dinner one night this week.

At Aunt Edie's, Mom meets us at the door.

"You, young lady," she says to me, "we need to talk." I wipe my boots on the dirty mat and avoid looking at her. Zelda pushes by me and hangs her jacket on a peg already covered with a puffy winter coat. It slips off and makes a knocking sound as the zipper hits the floor. Zelda keeps walking. Normally I would shout *Pick up your coat, dummy,* but instead I pick it up for her. I rearrange the other hanging coats so they are equally distributed on the other pegs. And then I re-hang Zelda's jacket.

"Here, Melinda, let me hang your coat for you," I offer.

"Thanks," she says. She passes her coat to me and follows after Zelda. Out of the corner of my eye, I see my mother cross her arms over her chest. She is shaking her head back and forth. I spend a few seconds rearranging the coats again.

Dad is holding the pizza boxes out in front of him. "Let me hold the pizza, Dad, so you can hang your coat up." Unfortunately, Dad's not wearing a coat. I hear Mom take a loud, deep breath.

"Aren't you being thoughtful." She doesn't try to hide her sarcasm. "You did a bad thing by sneaking that spider into the house!" she continues.

"I know. But I did tell you I was bringing the class pet home over vacation." I know that's a lame response but I can't think of anything else to say.

"Oh, that's funny, Jermaine," Mom says angrily. "I think you left out an important detail. You'll be punished for this," she tells me. A coat slips to the floor. I don't pick it up.

"I've been punished," I say, turning to face my mother. "Dad took away my camera." The camera hangs by its strap from my wrist. I grasp it with my hand.

"Really," she says. "What's that you're holding?"

"I gave it back to her," Dad interrupts. "We found the spider and it's out of the house."

"I know that. You told me that already." Mom sounds irritated with Dad, too. "But do you think she should be off the hook so soon? How about the total lack of respect she showed by sneaking that thing into the house in the first place? Not to mention letting it run wild!" Mom shudders.

"That's true," Dad says.

"I didn't mean to let it run *that* wild..." I say weakly.

"You know what I think," Mom asks but doesn't wait for me to answer, "I think you did it on purpose! I think this reality show of yours isn't turning out to be such a good idea, that's what I think. I think my sweet daughter is acting awfully sneaky these days!" I can't look my mother in the eye when she says that. Thankfully Aunt Edie walks into the room. "We'll discuss this later," Mom whispers angrily.

I turn to greet my aunt, who is holding her arms out to me. Her eyes look shiny and there are dark circles underneath them.

"Hi, Aunt Edie," I say. She squeezes me, resting her head on the side of my face. She smells musty, like hair that hasn't been washed lately. That surprises me and makes me sad for her because she usually smells like soap or something fresh out of the dryer. Her clothes look rumpled and she's not wearing any of her jewelry like she always does. The camera hangs from my wrist but I decide to leave it off.

"I made a salad," Aunt Edie says to no one in particular. "We'll have that and pizza." She releases me and smiles. I smile back. Then she lifts the boxes out of Dad's arms and shuffles back toward the kitchen. "Come. We'll eat soon," she says halfheartedly.

"Is she all right?" I ask. I'm hoping that my mother will put things in perspective and realize that a hairy spider is not such a big deal in comparison to what some other people are going through.

My mother ignores my question. "You are going to work this off, Jermaine. I will keep you very busy in the barn. You'll be cleaning jars and sorting cucumbers for the rest of your vacation and then some, you hear me?"

"My *whole* vacation?" Rufus Carmichael would never be caught slicing cucumbers or wearing a goofy hairnet. Famous people do not work in barns. Especially when they're on vacation! They have massages, and lounge by kidney-shaped pools. They sip fruity drinks with little plastic swords and paper umbrellas, and read magazines in hot tubs, and eat sushi. I try to stay calm. "I mean, that's a lot," I say.

"Well, then why don't I give you a choice?" Mom says.

"What do you mean?"

"You can work in the barn for the week or give up your camera for the week. You choose."

"That's some choice," I say angrily.

"That was some class pet." We stare at each other for

a few minutes before she says, "You choose," and then she walks into the kitchen.

I let the camera roll when I join the rest of my family. Zelda is filling glasses with ice cubes. Melinda carries several cans of soda to the table. One of the bulbs in the ceiling light is burned out, so it's dim. It looks as gloomy as it feels. There's a large stack of unopened mail, magazines, and several newspapers on the kitchen table. I can see that the blinds are open in the family room. I bet if it wasn't for Mom, they'd still be drawn. Not that it matters, it is dark outside anyways. Dad points to the pile of mail.

"Should we go through some of this after dinner?" he asks.

Aunt Edie nods, then says, "You spoke to Larry today."

"Yes," my father answers. She reaches for a can of soda and pulls the metal tab up with her finger. It hisses. Mom shakes the bottle of dressing. She opens it and pours some in a circle over the salad.

Aunt Edie takes a small sip from the can and swallows a burp. "I have news to tell you all," she announces. "Larry will be home tomorrow night." My mom looks up. The salad tongs are frozen in mid-toss. My parents give each other a look.

"Really," Melinda squeals, "tomorrow night?" Melinda knocks her fists together and bounces in her seat.

"Really." Aunt Edie looks across the table at my parents. She smiles. For a second I recognize her. "We'll celebrate with a homecoming party," she tells us.

Mom looks surprised. "Are you sure, Edie?"

"Larry will want to see everyone. He's missed us all." Aunt Edie sniffs and wipes a tear off her face. "Besides, he's very anxious to apologize." Then she lets out a sigh.

And the sad Edie reappears. I scan my camera around the table.

Zelda puts her hand on top of it and pulls it down. "Not now," she says softly.

Instead of telling her to mind her own business, I shut the camera off.

"That's fine," Mom is saying to Aunt Edie. "Whatever you want us to do. We are happy to come celebrate. You let us know when." She walks around the table and hugs her sister.

Then Dad joins them. Mom and Dad stand together with their arms around Aunt Edie. Melinda gets up to join them, too. I can hear someone softly crying. For a moment I wonder if I will cry. I've never seen my family like this before. Zelda gets up to join the group hug. I stand up. What do reality-show producers call a pivotal moment like this? Mrs. Finn calls it the climax of the story...or is it the resolution? What if Aunt Edie reveals the reason Uncle Larry ran away in the first place? Isn't this too important not to film? I turn the camera on but quickly shut it off. *Not now.* I step around the table to join the hug. Then before I do, I quietly move my camera to the top of the stack of mail, aim it at my family, and press record.

16
Pickles

If I ever get to be on that reality show *Trading Parents*, and get to swap families with another kid, my new parents would be lucky to have me. I make my bed almost every day. I wash the pots that are too big to fit in the dishwasher. I help shovel the walk after snowstorms. I know, most kids have chores to do around the house. But I dare anyone to find a kid who can pickle thirty pounds of cucumbers.

"All of these?" I ask my mother. I zoom in on the crates of cucumbers.

"Not all today," she tells me. "You have your whole vacation, remember? We'll need extra stock after the Palooza. I hope to have a big jump in sales." Then she points at me. "Put the camera down!" she orders. She hands me a hairnet and a pair of plastic gloves.

"Do I have to wear this thing?" I ask.

"You know it's the law, Jermaine," she tells me.

"Well, I think they should have a law against wearing

anything that makes you look like a geek." The plastic gloves are way too big for me. Mom carries another box of cucumbers out of the cold-storage room. She plops it onto the counter behind me.

"Use the Kirbys," she instructs. "Don't use the big ones. They don't belong in the dills." I carry the first batch of cucumbers to the sink. I carefully clean the miniature cucumbers with the spray hose, picking out and setting aside the oversized ones. The water sounds like a rainstorm as it gushes out the small holes of the colander and hits the bottom of the basin. I wonder how in the world I am going to get Uncle Larry on film when he comes home tonight. I never did record why he ran away in the first place. It was never brought up. But I did record my parents' look of utter horror when I asked Aunt Edie if I could come over and film Uncle Larry's return. And I have Zelda announcing that I'm an imbecile.

Sixty glass jars are spread across the top of the worktable in the pickling barn. It will take me all day to fill those jars! I know this because it's not the first time I've been sentenced to a day of pickling. If history is any indication of what the future holds, it may not be my last.

Two tall vats of brine heat up on the burners across the room. I'm glad I'm making dill pickles today. It's better than making the hot and spicy pickles, which need to be "chunked." That means slicing is involved. Slicing a gazillion cucumbers and hot peppers can get tedious...not to mention dangerous, especially if the juice of one of those peppers squirts in your eye. Forget the gloves and hairnet—you need safety glasses for those suckers.

"Remember, garlic first, then dill," Mom instructs me. "Each jar holds twelve or thirteen cucumbers, so don't short them!"

"What if I can only fit eleven?" I ask.

"I just told you what the jars hold, Jermaine. If you're only fitting eleven, you're using the wrong size cucumber!" she says.

"Okay, geez." *As if the world would come to an end if someone had eleven pickles instead of twelve!* "Can I phone a friend to help?" I ask hopefully. Mom sighs and rolls her eyes.

"This is not a social opportunity," she says. "You're being punished."

"Fine!" I leave the clean cucumbers in the sink and carry the garlic and dill over to the large center island. I drop a clove of garlic and some fresh dill weed into each open jar.

"I've got some Palooza stuff to do on the computer in the house. By the time I'm done, you should be finished filling the jars," she says. "I'll pour the brine, Jermaine. It's hot and I don't want you to burn yourself." I'm surprised she cares.

"Okay," I say. Mom grabs her coat and flings her scarf around her neck. When she slides the barn door shut, I pull the plastic gloves off my hands and toss them into the garbage pail. They are too big, and too annoying.

I continue stuffing the pickles into the jars, counting two, four, six, eight, ten, twelve, sometimes thirteen. Okay, sometimes eleven, but who's going to know? I wash another batch of cucumbers and repeat the process, counting, stuffing, washing until I am down to my last batch. After all the jars are complete, I add another clove of garlic and some more dill to each one. I've just finished the last jar when Mom returns to the barn.

"How's it going?" she asks. She smiles at me. I swear she hasn't smiled at me since the Harry episode yesterday.

She notices my hands right away, and her smile fades. "Where are your gloves?" she asks.

"I'm done," I tell her. "You just need to pour brine."

"Great job, Jermaine!" Mom gives me a hug. It feels like she's starting to like me again. "The labeling will have to wait until tomorrow," she tells me.

"Do I have to?" I ask.

"The jars need to cool before the labels can go on," she says.

"No, I mean do I really have to do this for my entire vacation?"

"You have to put the labels on. I'll date the stickers for the jars." Her voice is gentle. "If you start early tomorrow, you'll be done in just a couple of hours. And maybe," she winks at me, "I'll let you have the rest of the day off."

"Thanks, boss," I say. She laughs and gently taps her finger against the end of my nose.

"What time is Uncle Larry coming home tonight?" I ask.

"I don't know," she answers.

"Can I go over there to see him?" I ask. I figure I'll give it one last shot.

"I told you already, Jermaine, tonight is not the best time to visit," she says. "You'll see him Thursday night at the homecoming party."

But that's not the same thing, I want to say. Filming Uncle Larry when he first arrives home is not the same as filming him after all the drama has settled down. My viewers want to see when he first walks through the door. That's when all the good stuff is going to happen.

Mom washes her hands at the sink. She slips on a pair of gloves and a hairnet. I help her transfer the jars onto the rolling cart and push them over to the stove. While my mother ladles the brine, I put the garlic and dill away and wipe down the counters.

By six o'clock the jars are filled, the lids are on, and the water bath is done. Mom and I transfer the ready-to-be-pickled cukes to the cooling table. We'll leave them there overnight to properly seal. I am about to untie my apron when it dawns on me just how important it is to wear plastic gloves after all. I notice the lucky skull ring is no longer on my finger. I feel inside my apron pocket and search the floor around me. My heart pounds and it feels hot inside this chilly barn. My eyes scan the dozens of jars spread across the table. And I have a feeling—a sick, uneasy feeling—that Ro's ring is getting pickled, and what's left of my good luck is, too.

17
Pop

I have to wait for everyone in the house to fall asleep before I make my way down the dark staircase. I slide my foot slowly across each tread until I feel the edge of the step. It's a good thing Susie is a lousy watchdog. I hear her snoring softly at the other end of the hallway.

Downstairs by the back door, I grab any coat and wrap it around me. I slip my bare feet into a pair of furry boots. They must be Mom's because they feel too big.

The walk to the barn is short, but dark and cold. My flashlight makes a spot of light on the path in front of me. The sound of my own footsteps makes my heart race a bit faster and I pick up my pace. The trees look shadowy in the moonlight, their branches creaking slightly when the wind blows. The bushes, covered in frozen drifts of snow, remind me of ghosts. One of the few birds foolish enough not to fly south for the winter lets out a trill that makes me jump. I keep my eyes on the path. If there's something other than a bird out here, I don't want to know.

Inside the barn I flip on the light switch. The fluorescent tubes that run across the ceiling buzz softly as they flash. I gently stomp the snow off my boots and leave my coat on the floor. It feels warmer than usual in here. I check the thermostat on the wall. Mom must have forgotten to turn the heat down when we were done pickling.

Before I search for the ring, I film the jars on the table and scan the camera around the rest of the barn. At least if it's not that interesting for the reality show, it might be good for business.

I prop the camera on one of the shelves across from the cooling table, leaving it on so I can catch the moment I find that ring. Hopefully mom will think it's all pretty funny by the time she sees my show aired on TV. But what if I don't find it? What if a customer finds it in a jar of pickles instead? We'll get sued! Like Barbeque Bob, who had to pay some lady a million dollars after her husband almost chocked to death on the top of a pen that was in his coleslaw. What if someone choked on the skull ring? I'd have to go to prison! They'd definitely be able to trace the ring back to me. Anyone who knows my mom knows she's not the type to wear a skull ring, even for good luck. *Relax, Jermaine. Those dills have to pickle for weeks before they're ready to hit the stores. You have plenty of time to find that ring. And when you do, the proof will be right on film!*

I lift a jar up off the table and hold it above my head. Maybe it sank to the bottom. I turn it around, checking inside—nothing but pickles.

"One down, fifty-nine to go," I say. I check a second jar and then a third, but nothing. Then I hear *POP! POP! POP!* My heart tries to punch its way out of my chest. I can't breathe. But I quickly realize it's only the sound of the jars sealing. If I didn't have such extensive pickle experience, I would have hightailed it out of the barn. I probably would have even called the police.

Just as my heart starts to slow to a normal beat, the door to the storage room swings open and some weirdo flies out. I close my eyes and scream. Weirdo screams. I drop a jar of pickles and it smashes. *POP! POP! POP! POP!* The rest of the jars continue to pop, echoing through the barn. I stand, frozen in place, eyes shut, still screaming. Just when I run out of scream and I think I might have wet my pants (I find out later it was pickle juice), I hear someone shouting my name.

"Jermaine! Jermaine!" My eyes focus long enough to realize it's my long-lost Uncle Larry standing before me, wearing his penguin wings. I am desperately trying to breathe when he comes over and puts a flipper around me.

"Jermaine, it's me, Uncle Larry. It's okay." I'm still trying to catch my breath when he says: "What the heck is that racket? I thought someone was shooting up the place!" Uncle Larry holds his wings out. His hands poke out underneath through the arm holes, index fingers extended and thumbs up, like pretend guns. "BANG, BANG," he yells out, pointing his "guns" around the barn. "They're coming after me, I guess!" He laughs. It dawns on me that there might be something seriously wrong with my uncle. His normal self is weird, but the sight of him in those ridiculous penguin wings pretending to shoot up the place is pretty unsettling. Besides, you'd have to be crazy to come out and investigate if you really thought someone was shooting a gun...wouldn't you?

"Uncle Larry," I manage to say finally, "what are you doing here?"

"I should be asking you the same question," he says to me. "Isn't it past your bedtime?"

"I'm looking for something," I tell him.

"It isn't me, is it?"

"No, something else," I tell him. "Wait," I say as my brain tries to process the penguin wings and why he's here in the barn. "What are you doing here?" I ask again. "Aren't you supposed to be home?"

"I got cold feet," he tells me. Then he cracks his knuckles. He sighs. "Ever hear that saying, Jermaine?"

"Doesn't that apply to people who are getting married but change their minds?" I ask.

"Yes. But it applies to other events, too...bungee jumping...confronting an angry wife...you know what I mean?" I nod my head, but I'm a little confused. "I was all set to go home, but I got nervous, so here I am. I really have cold feet, too. It's freezing out tonight." Uncle Larry notices me staring at the penguin flippers he's wearing. He blushes as he lifts them up. "That's why I put these on," he explains. "They're cumbersome, but warm." He drops his arms back down to his sides. The flippers, curved and heavy-looking, hang like a couple of frowns. "By the way," he says, "your mother really needs to lock this place up. Her pickles are extremely tempting."

"Have you been staying here the whole time?" I ask. *Was he hiding out while I was working in the barn?* I imagine him crouched down behind the shelves watching me count cucumbers, sometimes only eleven.

"No, no," he tells me. "I did splurge a couple of times and stay at a motel. But the other nights I slept in my car. The heat isn't working so well in that old van tonight, so I figured I could stay here. I didn't expect to run into you. Sorry I scared you."

"Why did you leave?" I ask him. "Where have you

been?" Uncle Larry sighs again and his face gets very serious.

"I know it wasn't a nice thing to do, Jermaine. I know that. It was supposed to be a quick business trip but things didn't go the way I had planned." He shakes his head gently.

"It was a business trip? Why was it a secret?" I ask.

"It's complicated. Let me show you something," he tells me. He slips the wings off and leans them against the wall. Then he strides into the back room. When he comes out, he's holding an open jar of pickles. A bit of pickle juice splashes over the lip of the jar on his way back across the floor. He puts the jar down on the table and fishes two dills out with his fingers. "Have one," he offers.

"No, thanks." I notice something bulky sticking out from under his arm. It looks like a cloth bag. He wipes his fingers across his pants, reaches for the bag, and lays it down on the table. It's about the size of a magazine, slightly bigger.

"In here is my reason," he says slowly. "This is what it was all about," he whispers. He reaches into the sack. I didn't know what to expect. But I sure am surprised, not to mention more confused than ever, by what he pulls out of that bag.

18
The Glove

"I don't get it," I say. "A glove?"

"Not just any glove," Uncle Larry explains. "It's an electric balloon-fastening glue glove."

"Oh," I say.

"Have you ever been to Philadelphia?" he asks me.

"No."

"It's a beautiful city, tell your parents to take you there. Your Aunt Edie and I took Melinda two summers ago. Remember that?"

"I think so," I say hesitantly.

"Anyhow," he continues, "in Centre Square there's a forty-five-foot-tall clothespin." He leans across the table toward me. "It's FASCINATING!" he bellows. "It's supposed to resemble a couple kissing, but I don't see it." That makes me blush, and Uncle Larry notices. "I'm getting off track, aren't I?"

He slips his hand inside the glove and gazes at it. He holds it out in front of me and turns it from side to side.

An electrical cord hangs from the wrist of the glove and knocks against the table. "When I saw that giant clothespin I couldn't help but think about balloons," he tells me. "How wonderful to have a giant balloon, maybe in the shape of a T-shirt or a pair of pants, clamped atop that wonderful clothespin. I bet the artist who designed that sculpture never imagined that!" He pauses for a few seconds. I don't know what to say. "It gave me the idea for a new way to fasten a balloon!" he says excitedly. "After our trip, I created some mini clothespins. I used all of our savings to make those pins. Ten thousand I had made! Instead of tying the balloons, I would use the mini pins to close them. But the balloon animals and bouquets were a problem. The edges of the plastic pins were popping the balloons. It was a big fiasco. And afterward, Aunt Edie made me promise never to spend our money on any more of my ideas. But I knew there had to be a better way to fasten a balloon. If only I could figure it out, I could turn the balloon industry on its ear!" He is practically shouting.

"What's wrong with just tying the balloon? Why would anyone want to use a glue glove?" I ask. "No offense," I add.

"Why wash dishes by hand if you can use a dishwasher? Why use a non-powered screwdriver if you have a powered one? Why whip cream with a whisk if you can whip it up with an electric mixer?"

"I get it," I tell him. "You can fasten more balloons with the glue glove?"

"Right! It's called efficiency!" he says proudly. I remember at the Fourth of July dinner Uncle Larry had used that same word. "I drove to Aroostook County to get the glove," he tells me.

"Aroostook County!" I say. "That's practically in Canada!" I didn't want to point out that it might have been more efficient to have the thing mailed. As if he can read my mind, Uncle Larry explains.

"After the mini clothespin disaster, I had to be sure the glove worked. Remember that phone call the night I left, the balloon delivery to the senior home?" I nod. "It was really the man who made the glove. He called to confirm our meeting later that night."

"But why did you have to meet in the night?"

"I left that night to pick up the glove because I had to act fast," my uncle explains. "Edie had planned to buy the van the next Monday. I was running out of time. It had to be a secret because of the promise I had made her... see? But I figured if I could *show* her how great the glove worked, she'd be excited about it. So I left to pick up the glove. I drove back home late that same night. I knew Edie and Melinda would be asleep. My plan was to fill up all of the rooms downstairs with balloons. In the morning Edie would see with her own eyes that the glove was a great idea. She'd forget all about the money I used up to have it made." Uncle Larry rubs his eyes. "And she'd realize my idea was better than a second van," he says softly.

Then Uncle Larry takes the glove off and slams it roughly onto the table.

"What are you doing?" I gasp. "Don't break it!"

"It doesn't matter. The darn thing doesn't work," he says wearily.

"It doesn't work?"

"Well, it starts out okay, see?" He shows me a small hole at the tip of one of the fingers.

"When you turn the glove on, the glue comes out here at the index finger." Uncle Larry finds an outlet next to the table and plugs in the cord. "Watch." He points to a bead of glue that appears on the fingertip of the glove. "This goes inside the neck of the balloon. Then you squeeze the neck like this." Uncle Larry pinches his thumb and middle finger together. "But the longer you use the glove, the hotter it gets," he says, shaking his head. "It heats the glue and the neck of the balloon and melts it. What a mess!" He yanks the cord roughly out of the wall.

"But—" I start to say.

"It worked fine when I tested it up in Presque Isle. But back at home, after I used the glove on seven or eight balloons, they all started to melt. I immediately drove back up north hoping the guy could work out the kinks. I suggested changing around the wires inside or adding a lining that would protect the fingers of the glove from getting too hot. But nothing worked." Uncle Larry shakes his head.

I wasn't sure what to say to that. "At least you gave it a shot," I offer.

"I spent every single penny we saved up for the second van." He sighs. "Now I have a glove that doesn't work and no money for a van. I messed up! I didn't mean to be gone so long. The longer it took me to try to fix it, the harder it got for me to come home. Then she discovered the money was gone...she's very mad. On top of that I broke my promise. She might never forgive me."

"Can't you get your money back?" I ask him.

"Nope, I can't." Uncle Larry's eyes shine. "It cost the man who made it for me a lot of money...and a whole lot more to try to fix it. The glove was my idea...not his...that's the way it goes with inventions...no guarantees!"

"You were planning a surprise," I remind him. "If you explain that to Aunt Edie, maybe she won't be so mad." At first I think he's laughing at me, which seems odd. But then he holds his head in his hands. His shoulders are jumping up and down, and I hear a strange noise like an animal sound. It's a wail. He's sobbing. I have never seen my uncle cry. I wonder what I'm supposed to do. I try to remember what Mom does to make me feel better when I cry. She usually hugs me, or rubs my back. Sometimes she gives me a cookie. Should I offer him a pickle?

"It will be okay, Uncle Larry," I say, trying desperately to cheer him up. "It's not like you lost the money on purpose...it's the thought that counts."

"I shouldn't have done what I did," he mumbles. "I keep screwing up! I'm supposed to be home right now." He sniffs.

"Well, you can still keep *that* promise. The day isn't over yet." I point to the clock behind him. He looks over his shoulder. With the back of his hand he wipes his eyes.

"You're right, Jermaine." He smiles a little. "I'm going home now." He leans forward and kisses me on the forehead. "Thanks for listening to me." He pats my arm, then shuffles toward the door, snatching up his black-and-white wings on the way. "Good night," he calls out. A gust of winter wind howls when he steps outside.

"Good night," I say. But the sound of the wind and the sliding barn door muffle my words. And before I can say it again, he's gone.

In the storage room I find a broom next to the shelves of pickles. I sweep up the broken glass. I gather the open jar of dills and an empty one Uncle Larry must have finished. I toss everything out and wipe up the spilled juice. My body feels heavy and slow.

I wonder if Dad has ever cried like Uncle Larry did tonight. If so, would I have had the guts to reach out and rub his back? Uncle Larry seems different now. Not bad different, just different. And that makes everybody else seem different, too. My parents, Aunt Edie, even Zelda. Tonight *I* feel like the older sister. I'm not sure I like it.

I put the broom away. I almost forget about my camera. It sits on the shelf still recording. It reminds me that I was able to get Uncle Larry's homecoming after all. Even without the lucky skull ring. Speaking of that, I've barely started to look for it. It will have to wait until tomorrow. I'm not up to it now.

I reach for the camera and press the stop button. After I grab my coat, I turn the heat down and flick the light switch off. The barn door feels heavier than usual when I slide it closed behind me. And the walk back to the house seems darker and colder than before.

19
Are You Awake, Mr. Carmichael?

Dear Mr. Carmichael,

I am writing this letter at midnight because I can't sleep. But it's only 9:00 out in Hollywood. You're probably at a party right now with some other celebrities.

Did I ever mention my disappearing uncle? He split a little over a week ago, and no one knew why. Tonight the mystery of Uncle Larry has been solved. I captured the 411 for my reality show! I was in the pickle barn looking for a skull ring (I'd tell you about that, but you'd probably never buy a jar of Nora's Pickles if I do). It turns out Uncle Larry was in the barn hiding. He left to get a glue glove made for the balloon business he owns with Aunt Edie. It didn't work out well at all. He spent all their money and my aunt is really mad. My uncle is very sad about everything. He cried.

Lately the footage for my show has been much better. The thing is, my stomach hurts a lot. Is that a common side effect among reality-show producers? Has this ever happened to you?

Looking forward to hearing back from you.

Sincerely,
"You know who!"

PS Have you given any more thought to my suggestion about The Country Life? You and I would make a great team!

20

New Beginnings

New Beginnings is the theme for tonight's welcome-home party at my aunt and uncle's house.

"I think it's lovely!" Mom clasps her hands together. Dad sweeps the ashes out of the fireplace. I zoom in on the little black smudge above his eyebrow.

"I think they should celebrate Larry's homecoming privately," Dad says, dumping a pan of ashes into a tin pail.

"Why would you say that?" Mom asks.

"I'm glad everything's worked out between them, of course, but do we need to be involved?" he asks. "Isn't this a private matter?"

"Nobody's getting involved in anything. We're going to celebrate," Mom says happily.

Aunt Edie was so relieved to have Uncle Larry home she wasn't angry anymore. Three days ago, on Monday, the morning after Uncle Larry had finally come home, Mom spoke to Aunt Edie on the phone. Zelda and I quickly ran upstairs and listened in on another extension. I had to pretend some of the stuff I heard was news to me since I didn't want to spill the beans on Uncle Larry's cold feet and our meeting in the barn the night before. He didn't snitch on me, either, because Aunt Edie never mentioned it. In fact, he must have left the whole hiding-in-the-barn part out completely. I only hope I don't get blamed for the missing jars of pickles.

"I was afraid this had to do with that ridiculous glove idea of his," Aunt Edie groaned through the phone. "After the mini clothespin disaster, I didn't think he'd dare." Since Uncle Larry agreed to sell his prized pop-up camper to recover some of the van money, Aunt Edie forgave him. "He means well, he really does."

"We don't need to wear a costume to this homecoming party, do we?" Dad is asking. He wipes his sooty hands on a rag.

"Do we?" Zelda asks. She pours chocolate chips into a bowl of cookie dough.

"No costume," Mom says. "But we each need to bring something that symbolizes a new beginning. A fresh flower, maybe?" she suggests.

"Where are we supposed to get a flower in the dead of winter?" Dad asks.

"Oh for heaven's sake, use your imagination!" Mom tells him. "We can get one at the grocery store, or the girls can make them out of tissue paper."

"Well, hopefully this new beginning will be the end of Larry's crazy ideas," Dad says.

"I think that's the plan," Mom agrees. Dad hangs the little fireplace broom back on the stand and carries the bucket of ashes out to the garage when he leaves for work. Zelda finishes baking cookies for the homecoming party tonight, and Mom and I trek out to the pickling barn.

"I'll help pack the pickles," I tell my mother. I am hoping to search for Ro's ring, which I still haven't found—not even when I labeled the jars the day after I ran into Uncle Larry. I haven't looked for the ring since. Mom was with me in the barn all day Tuesday, and yesterday she let me off the hook so I could go skiing with Nina and her family.

"I've packed the pickles," she says, flipping the light on.

"All of them?" I ask.

"Honey, the Pickle Palooza starts tomorrow and we have Larry's party tonight. I don't want to be up late packing pickles," she says. "The dills, hot-and-spicies, pickled veggies, bread-and-butters, and piccalilli are all set. I only have a few jars of the pickled red pepper relish," Mom says as she reaches for a small box, "a jar for the judges and a couple more for sampling. That'll work, you think?"

"That sounds good to me," I say. *Though I'm only an expert when it comes to reality shows, not pickles.*

"I don't have labels for the relish yet," Mom continues. "I won't sell a product without a label. It doesn't look right." She places the box on the table. "We need to pack the sample serving cups and tasting spoons, and my tablecloth, too." Mom dodges around the barn opening cabinets and drawers. "Oh, and napkins!"

"I'll get the relish for you," I tell her. I sprint into the storage room.

"Thank you, Jermaine," she says.

Inside the tiny storage room the walls are covered with shelving from floor to ceiling. There are hundreds of jars of my mother's pickle products. I search the shelves where the dills are stacked. I am surrounded by images of my mother's smiling face wrapped around all of these jars. She won't be smiling when she discovers a skull in her pickles.

"What's taking you so long?" The sound of Mom's voice makes me jump. She laughs. "Sorry! Didn't mean to scare you! The relish is over here, silly. Let me help you carry out the jars." Then something dawns on me. *Maybe the ring isn't in the pickles,* I tell myself hopefully. Maybe it's somewhere else. Maybe it got washed down the drain. Maybe I have nothing to even worry about. It's possible. Anything is possible, I suppose.

In the evening at Uncle Larry and Aunt Edie's, we gather in the den after dinner. A fire roars in the fireplace. I wonder if Uncle Larry will toss the glove into the flames as a symbol that he's done with his crazy invention ideas once and for all. But he doesn't. I am able to zoom in on the burning logs before my mom tells me to put the camera away.

"For heaven's sake, by all means keep on filming," Aunt Edie tells me. "This is a momentous occasion that should be recorded. Besides, what do all famous show-biz folks say...the show must go on!" Dad looks at Mom. "It's a party! A celebration! Roll the camera!" Aunt Edie says.

"I suppose when Jermaine is ready to have her family showing, this will be nice to see," Mom says hesitantly.

"The whole world is going to see this!" I tell her. Dad and Uncle Larry laugh.

"Let's not get too carried away," Mom says gently. I notice the skin on Uncle Larry's forehead is shiny. I wonder if he's nervous or if it's the heat from the fire.

"Let's get started," Aunt Edie says.

One by one we place our tokens of new beginnings on

the coffee table. Zelda and I each lay a rose that we bought at the grocery store in the center of the table. Mom holds an egg. She places it in a small bowl before she puts it down so it won't roll off. Dad holds up an unopened bottle of glass cleaner.

"It's brand-new...never been opened," he boasts. He plunks it next to the roses.

"So bizarre," Zelda whispers.

"I have this," Melinda smiles. She opens a black book and fans through its empty white pages. "It's a new journal," she tells us, sliding it onto the table. Aunt Edie and Uncle Larry together have a new bottle of sparkling apple cider and a fancy glass for everyone. Uncle Larry makes a toast.

"To my family," he says, holding his empty glass, "Edie, Melinda, Nora, Clark, Zelda, and Jermaine." He pauses for a moment while he looks at each of us. Then he continues. "I am so happy to be home and I am so very sorry that I worried you. Thank you for forgiving me." Uncle Larry's voice cracks. "I love you all," he says, sweeping his arm out in front of him. I focus the camera on Aunt Edie. She pats Uncle Larry's shoulder. Melinda wraps her thin arms around her father's thick waist.

Then Uncle Larry fills up everyone's glass.

"To new beginnings!" he says loudly. There's clinking and more cries of "To new beginnings!" Uncle Larry catches my eye and winks. I smile back at him. I decide at that moment that once I become rich and famous I'll buy Uncle Larry the biggest and best pop-up camper he's ever seen. We sip the fizzy apple drink. There's a long, awkward stretch of silence.

"Let's clean up from dinner and have dessert," Mom says. "Zelda made chocolate chip cookies."

"And I've got a lemon sponge cake," Aunt Edie tells us, "and fruit cocktail." Everyone helps. I film Aunt Edie as she slips the dishes neatly between the prongs of the dishwasher. My mom dries a large roasting pan with a towel and Zelda and Melinda spoon leftovers into Tupperware. Louise walks along the kitchen counter and I zoom in on Dad shaking his head in disgust.

"Jermaine isn't helping," Zelda announces. "As usual, she only cares about her camera and getting *famous.*" She pumps her index and middle fingers into quotation marks.

"Jermaine," my mother says, "put the cookies on a plate and find some more napkins."

"Nora," my aunt says, "are you ready for the Palooza?"

"I am," Mom tells her.

"You girls will be there Friday night to help?" my aunt asks over her shoulder. "Melinda is going to help us decorate your booth. We found some wonderful Mylar balloons...green pickles!"

"You're kidding!" Mom laughs.

"I read in the newspaper there's going to be a mystery judge," Aunt Edie tells Mom.

"Yes, I heard," Mom answers. "I wonder who."

"We'll find out tomorrow night."

"Hopefully he or she likes pickled red pepper relish!" Dad adds.

"I think it deserves first prize," Uncle Larry says. "By the way, do you have enough business cards for the two days?"

"Oh yes," Mom answers. "I printed out a whole bunch on the computer." I arrange the cookies on a plate. I should consider business cards for myself. I am positive famous reality-show producers carry them. My cards will have to be huge to fit all my titles. Jermaine Davidson: director, creator, producer, camera person, guest star...my phone number, I'll probably have several, and my address, I may have several of those, too. And I'll definitely have an email address so my fans and other really famous people can reach me easily. Unlike Rufus Carmichael, who obviously hasn't bothered to read his mail.

Back at home, Mom tells us to have an early night.

"We have two very busy days and we need to be bright-eyed and all smiles starting tomorrow afternoon!"

Upstairs in my room, I place my camera on my desk. Before I have a chance to get undressed there's a knock on my door.

"This is the first time today I've had a chance to check the mail," Mom says, poking her head around the door frame. She holds out her arm. A letter is pressed between her fingers. "This looks important." She winks at me. I snatch the letter out of her hand. "Good for you, Jermaine. I'm so impressed! What a savvy girl you are, seeking advice from a big-time producer for your little reality show!" Mom blows a kiss and leaves.

Little reality show?

The return address looks fancy. The letters and numbers are white like the envelope, and are stiff and bumpy, but easy to read. My first thought is, *Rufus Carmichael's famous fingers touched this envelope.* Then, with trembling hands, I open the letter.

21
Dear Jermaine

Dear Jermaine,

It was very nice to hear from you. I wish you lots of luck with your reality show. Starting at such a young age I have no doubt one day you will be successful if you stick with it.

The best advice I can give you is to follow your dream. If producing reality-TV shows is what you are passionate about, I encourage you not to give up. The TV business can be difficult, but also very rewarding.

Thank you for your suggestion for The Country Life. We are always searching for new locations.

You never know, perhaps our paths will cross one day soon. It would be a pleasure to meet you.

Please be well.

Yours very truly,

Rufus Carmichael

22
Palooza

"You did not!" Nina shrieks excitedly.

"Did too!" I shriek back.

"What's it say?" Melinda asks.

"That my show is going to be a huge success!" I hand Nina the letter.

"Really!" Nina holds the letter so Melinda can see, too. I watch their eyes dart back and forth over the page.

"This is so awesome," Melinda squeals.

"Don't tear it or get it dirty," I warn. Nina holds the letter gently, touching only the very edges. "See where it says I'm going to be a great success, because I'm so young? I knew it," I tell them. "I knew I'd be doubly famous because of my age." I film the two of them reading the letter. Imagine! Rufus Carmichael has a part in *my* show. His letter to me, anyway...just being able to use his name...I feel myself getting more famous by the minute!

"Girls, you're here to help, right?" my father reminds us. I turn the camera onto Dad. He's unpacking jars and stacking them in a pyramid on top of the table. Mom's yellow checked cloth for special events covers the tabletop and hangs just above the floor. A brass easel holds a sign. NORA'S PICKLES is scrolled in bold black letters across the top, and the assorted products from her pickle line are listed underneath. At the bottom of the sign is my mother's smiling face, the same happy face from the labels.

Aunt Edie and Uncle Larry fasten green balloons onto the legs of the easel, and a cascade of curled white and silver ribbon spills down the sides of the sign. A tall bouquet of shiny Mylar balloons shaped like pickles is anchored to the corner of the table behind the pyramid of jars. A special weight is tied to the end of the ribbons to keep the balloons from floating away.

"We're coming!" I say to Dad. I carefully refold the letter and slip it back inside the envelope. I tuck it inside the long zippered pocket on the outside of my jacket where it will be safe. Zelda and Katrina organize the little sample cups and spoons. I pan my camera around the room. There sure are a lot of pickle-makers here. They've come from all over...some from as far as Colorado, but mostly from Maine or other parts of New England.

The community room inside the Penobscot River Inn is lined with rows of tables. All pickle-makers have their own square space just like ours, separated by walls that are basically white curtains pulled taut and held steady by metal poles.

"Do you want to unpack the brochures and business cards?" Mom asks me. She chops pickles on a plastic board into sample-sized pieces. "They're over there." She points with her chin to some open cartons. Mom wears a yellow apron that matches the cloth on the table. Her red curls are pulled back away from her face and sit in a springy mound on the top of her head.

"Okay," I tell her. I find the brochures and cards in one of the smaller boxes. "Fan them out like this." I show Melinda and Nina. On the other side of the room near the back entrance is a food court. The smell of something yummy makes me hungry. I see a popcorn machine from where I stand, and a sign for baked beans and brown bread. There's pizza, too. I saw it when we came in the back exit from the parking lot. It's right next to where Uncle Larry left his extra helium tank.

At three o'clock, the doors open to the public. The Winter Pickle Palooza has officially begun! Right away the room is crowded and starting to feel hot. All of us will take turns "working the booth"—handing out samples, business cards, and brochures. Aunt Edie and Uncle Larry offer free balloons imprinted with *Nora's Pickles* to the passersby. There are people everywhere. Some come to taste, some to buy. Grocers seek out new products for their stores.

"This is a wonderful turnout!" Mom gushes to Dad.

Later on, Mrs. Fairly, Nina's mom, pushing Granny Viola in her wheelchair, stops by the booth to say hi.

"Hello, Viola." Mom reaches out and holds Granny V's hands. She looks up at Mrs. Fairly. "The girls have been a great help. I was just going to suggest they walk around and get something to eat."

Mrs. Fairly turns to look at the food court. "Mother," she says to Granny Viola, "let me get you some supper."

"I just ate," Granny V answers. Mrs. Fairly gives Mom a sad look and shakes her head.

"No, Mother, you didn't," she tells her.

"Didn't I?" Granny Viola frowns. "What time is it?"

"It's okay. We can wait if you're not hungry."

"She gets confused sometimes," Nina whispers. I rub Granny Viola's shoulder gently.

Mom hands money to Zelda and Katrina. "Here," she says to me, pushing a twenty-dollar bill into my hand, "you treat." Zelda and Katrina head off to the food area.

"Let's get some stuff first," I say to Nina and Melinda. We stop at each booth, collecting free key rings, rubber jar openers, pencils, and magnets, all with different pickle-maker logos. We taste-test the competition: sours and half-sours, sweet gherkins, Polish dills, German dills, and kosher dills.

"I like these," Melinda says, dangling a bread-and-butter chip over her mouth.

"I don't like sweet pickles, I only like sour," Nina tells us. There are piccalillis; most, in case you didn't know, do not contain a single pickle. There are relishes, some sweet and some spicy, but none with red peppers. The Palooza is fun to film, but I must be careful not to overdo it...my reality show is about my family. I don't want this to come off like a pickle documentary.

By the time we finish tasting all the pickle products, we're not at all hungry.

"I don't think I'll eat another pickle as long as I live!" Nina tells us. "The inside of my mouth is all puckery."

"Mine too," Melinda says.

Back at the booth, a crowd stands in front of Mom's table. Aunt Edie is passing out brochures and Dad is spooning samples into the little white cups. Melinda and I inflate balloons, while Nina and Uncle Larry hand them out.

An hour or so of this and I'm thinking about asking Mom if we can hitch a ride home with Nina's mother. But suddenly, there's a commotion at the front of the room. Two men, each holding a TV camera on his shoulder, wait by the doors.

"What's going on?" I ask. Mom looks toward the cameras.

"The TV news is here...the mystery judge is arriving!"

"Where?" Melinda asks, standing on her tiptoes.

"Who is it?" Aunt Edie asks excitedly. Then a voice booms over the loudspeaker.

"Ladddddddiiiies and Gennnttttlemen...pickkkkllllle maaaaaakerrrrrrs and pickkkkllllle loverrrrrrrrs"— there's laughing and then more booming voice—"the Paloooooooooza mystery judge has arrrrrrrrived..." The door swings open and several men in long dark coats enter. Whoever it is must be important. The mystery judge has an entourage! I stuff the balloon I'm holding and about to inflate into my front pocket and reach for my camera lying on a box.

In the center of the "posse" is another man. The crowd recognizes him and bursts into cheers and applause. It's the mystery judge, and he's wearing a dark hat. It's not a baseball hat or a ski hat. It's soft with a dent on the top and a rim like a cowboy's hat, but smaller. He raises his arm and waves to the cheering crowd. His leather-gloved hand, shiny and important-looking, turns from side to side. The crowd is excited and noisy. I focus the camera on the back of his hat. A swarm of people continue to shuffle to the center of the room. Dad stretches his neck up to see over the crowd.

"He must be pretty famous, this place is going wild!" Aunt Edie announces. All of a sudden I freeze. I feel a pounding sensation against the inside of my stomach and up into my chest. The room starts to sway. My brain is pedaling faster than I can keep up with it. Thoughts spin furiously—a whirlwind that forces me to catch my breath. They come at me like a pounding rainstorm, one heavy drop after another...an important-looking man, an entourage, TV cameras...a small town...Dear Jermaine...hope to cross paths...someday soon...

"Rufus Carmichael!" I shout. The secret judge! He's here to scope out the location for *The Country Life* reality show! What could be more country-like than this Pickle Palooza...and the Penobscot River Inn! Not to mention the fact that my mother makes her pickles in a *barn*! I know I mentioned that in my letter! "Mr. Carmichael!" I shout louder.

"Are you SURE?" Nina bellows. "Is it really him?" Her eyes practically bug out of her head.

"What are you talking about, Jermaine?" Uncle Larry asks.

"It has to be him! It makes sense! Let me by!" I say. Uncle Larry shifts over into the curtain wall. "Let me by, let me by!" I squeal. But there's not enough room. I rush around to the other end of the table. "MOM!" I yell. "Push over! Let me out!"

"What's with you, Jermaine? Stop it! Everyone's trying to see," she scolds. The aisles are filled with people trying to get a look at the mystery judge. The throng blocks the front of our booth. Holding my camera above me in one hand, I place my other hand on Mom's shoulder and squeeze myself between her and the table. I hop up a bit so I'm half sitting on the table's edge. "Jermaine, what on earth...?" my mother yells over her shoulder. I continue to inch my way sideways. "The pickles!" Mom cries. When I reach the corner of the table, I push off with all of my might into the crowd. I feel the front edge of the table dip downward. The next thing I hear is a loud thud and the sound of glass clinking together and then frantic voices behind me. I look over my shoulder. Mom is desperately trying to catch the pyramid of jars sliding to the floor. Dad grabs for the tipped table while Aunt Edie and Uncle Larry, stuck on the other side, watch helplessly. A couple standing nearby reach out to help. Nina and Zelda yell to me but I turn away. I must get to Rufus Carmichael!

I squeeze myself into the thick crowd, rotating my body from side to side. My shaky legs carry me slowly and steadily toward the center of the room. The cameras are just ahead. Their lights make a golden circle around Rufus Carmichael. To think, he's just steps away! I hug my camera to my chest. Wait until he sees my reality show! I'll be famous by tomorrow...Sunday at the latest. I continue to weave and jostle my way through the crowd.

"Watch out! Please! Let me through!" I say. "Mr. CAR-MICHAEL!" I scream. "MR. CARMICHAEL!" I see his hat just ahead of me. I recognize the dark hair poking out the sides from magazine photos. He turns just enough so I can see his profile. He looks much younger in person. I am steps away when he turns completely around and faces me. I stop. My camera slips out of my hand. It clatters to the floor. This can't be. The mystery judge looks younger than my dad. Mr. Carmichael is as old as my grandfather.

Then somebody standing next to me calls him *Governor.*

23
Release

I am so close to the governor I can reach out and touch him. But I don't. I feel my jaw drop. My mouth hangs open. The governor smiles my way, and then turns to shake someone's hand. A lady holding a microphone steps in front of me.

"Pardon," she says, "I need to get in here." My feet stay bolted to the floor, and she steps around me. My brain is so busy being confused it doesn't tell my body to move out of the way, or to run from embarrassment. Or that I am an idiot. But that changes quickly. I reach down for my camera, in front of me and wedged between somebody's dirty boots. I have to yank and twist it free.

"What the...?" The man with the boots turns and gives me a nasty look.

The crowd begins to thin out as I make my way back to the booth. What a stupid idea to have a mystery judge. Who invited the *governor*? Doesn't he have more governer-ish things to do? Besides, a politician should be impartial to things like who makes the best pickle product.

Ahead of me I see my mom kneeling, her back hunched and her arms busy. The table is sloped to the ground, like a seesaw, one end up, the other down, with one of the corners resting on a crushed cardboard box underneath it. The shiny pickle balloons, now anchored to the floor, sway and knock each other. Aunt Edie, Uncle Larry, and Dad rifle through a mess of broken glass. Something red and lumpy soaks into the stiff carpeting. My head is light. It feels too big for my shoulders. Mom's relish is splattered all over the place. Her prizewinning product is a stain in the carpet. I don't see Melinda or Nina anywhere, but Zelda and Katrina walk around the broken table, checking out the damage, their heads tipped at an angle. A man in denim overalls arrives. His whiskered face is serious, and he carries a large roll of shiny silver tape and some kind of metal tool.

I did this. I ruined Mom's display, her relish, and her chance to win first place. Regret shimmies up the back of my throat. I try to swallow it but everything inside me feels tight and broken. Then before anyone can notice me, I run toward the food court. My eyes, foggy with tears, are almost useless as I search for an empty table. I scoot underneath one, tucking myself out of sight thanks to the scratchy tablecloth that reaches the floor. I sit on the hard carpet and hug my knees so the seam of my pants presses through my shirt sleeve and into my skin. With my tongue I catch a tear that has come to rest on my top lip. I sit for a long time, invisible to everyone and barely breathing.

I push rewind on my camera. The disk works its way backward to the beginning. I press play.

I watch Mom clean chicken and a few minutes of the

scene on the Stairmaster. I fast-forward to Zelda eating lasagna, Susie licking the plate, Dad straightening out the pantry—ordinary stuff. Then Zelda screams as the microwave shoots out flames. There's Aunt Edie marching in front of the stove at the Fourth of July dinner, singing and poking at those bobbing hot dogs; Melinda and her tattoos hanging out in her bathing suit; Uncle Larry counting rolls; Mom in shorts dripping wet and shivering, her teeth chattering; Dad smashing his head on the table; Uncle Larry picking his teeth. Celebrating the Fourth of July in the middle of February is weird.

Here's the mini hair salon scene. Zelda stomps out of the bathroom. Ro cries. Her hair is terrible and her nose is running.

"Shut it off already, Jermaine," I whisper at the little screen. I skip over more ordinary stuff, Melinda in the pet aisle at Walmart, then eating kung pao chicken. I stop at Harry the tarantula. Mom looks crazy. I wonder what her customers would think seeing the pickle lady flipping her lid like that. They'd be shocked to hear those bad words flying out of the same smiling mouth they see on the Nora's Pickles labels. I watch Melinda cry by the cans of paint, missing her father. I can't watch this part. I fast-forward some more. There's Aunt Edie. She was so sad and I was filming her in her rumpled clothes. Here's the scene in the barn last Sunday night. Why did I film myself searching for that ring? Maybe the ring *didn't* end up in a jar of Mom's pickles. But the whole world watching this would think that it did! There's Uncle Larry eating pickles and waving his arms. He talks about the giant clothespin. He slams the glove on the table. He's bawling. His bald spot takes up part of the screen while he leans his head into his hands and sobs. I cringe when I watch this scene. My Uncle Larry, who's always cheery and coming up with silly ideas and funny balloon animals, seems so *un*-Uncle Larry. I wonder what he'd think if he saw himself like this on TV—or even worse, if he knew I was filming him the whole time.

My audience might think my family is funny—not *ha-ha* funny, but *strange* funny. And I was worried my family was *too* ordinary. I guess there's an upside to being ordinary.

I fast-forward to tonight. Mom sets up for the Pickle Palooza. Dad arranges the jars, my aunt and uncle decorate with balloons. They found those special pickle-shaped balloons just for the Palooza. Mom is waving and smiling at the camera. Her apron is so yellow it looks happy—if that's possible for an apron.

I shut the camera off. For a split second I imagine myself stretched out on a cushy leather seat inside a limo. I'm sipping Sprite from the can, and wearing sunglasses even though the windows are tinted. But then I see Uncle Larry's crying face; Aunt Edie's wrinkled clothes; Mom's flapping arms; Ro's runny nose; the tumbling pyramid of pickles. It's like a TV screen flashing image after image inside my head. The scenes play over and over again, so fast I feel my heart beating to catch up with them. Now there's sound. Mom is screaming. Melinda is crying. Uncle Larry is sobbing. The jars are breaking. Right now, I am the opposite of famous. I'm somebody nobody wants to know.

I reach up to wipe my wet face with the back of my sleeve. My brain is quiet. Then it starts again. But this time it's not a playback from my reality show. It's my own voice inside my head. It says that my reality show doesn't tell the whole truth about my family. And it doesn't tell the whole truth about me, either.

I flop over onto my stomach, careful so my legs don't poke out and give me away. I lift the hem of the cloth. There's a long line waiting at the food counter. To the right and behind the pizza stand I see the tank of helium next to the back door. I pick up my camera and hold it in my hands. With my thumb I push down on the square button. The little door opens and I pop the disk inside it out. I feel for the balloon I know is still in my front pocket. I push the disk into the mouth of the balloon, tugging at the stretchy rim and squeezing it through the neck until it falls into its rubbery belly. Holding it tightly in my fist, I crawl out from under the table, leaving my camera behind. I sprint toward the helium tank. In less than a minute, the balloon is inflated and tied. My reality show is safe inside.

I push the heavy metal door with my shoulder and step outside. The door clanks shut and the frosty night air bites at me. Above the parking lot the moon hangs like a lost balloon in the sky.

Pale moonlight spills onto the tops of the cars. A frozen field beyond shines like a sparkling white ocean, the Paul Bunyan statue looming like a massive, dark cloud in the center of it.

From outside I hear the buzz of the Palooza. The table is probably fixed now. The unbroken jars, if there are any, have been restacked. Somebody, I'm sure, is looking for me.

The wind tugs at the balloon between my palms. It's eager for me to let it go. I open my hands and release it. The balloon spins into the night, silently, like a secret. The winter air blows and lifts it higher, carrying it over the parking lot. It pitches left, then right, sailing toward the river, up above bare treetops and, finally, out of sight.

24
Little Stuffers

From my bedroom window I see the light in the barn. I imagine my mother working furiously to make more red pepper relish.

By the time Zelda found me sitting by the information booth, the Palooza was closed for the night and the place was mostly empty.

"Your life as you know it is over," she told me. I refused to move out of the metal folding chair, but Zelda grabbed me by the arm and yanked me up. "You've caused enough trouble. Come on. Everyone wants to go home." My aunt and uncle were kind enough not to hang around while I got yelled at by my parents. They scrammed once they knew I hadn't run away, offering to drop Katrina and Nina at home. Dad did most of the yelling. Mom was too upset and disappointed to say much of anything. She could hardly look at me. When we got home I was sent straight to my room not knowing what was in store for me in the way of punishment. My parents hadn't figured that out yet. The crashing table did not qualify under Aunt Edie's "no crying over spilled milk" rule. This was different.

I left my camera under the table at the Palooza. When someone finds it I will not claim it from the lost and found. Maybe the person who does find it will keep it. It doesn't matter. My career in reality TV is over. My show is on its way to Canada. Or depending on which way the wind blows, maybe France or China, if it makes it across the ocean. I hope it gets lost at sea forever.

My stomach growls from hunger, but I don't feel like eating. I can't sleep, either. I hug my pillow and let my face fall forward. The tears soak into the pillowcase, and I sit up to wipe my cheeks and nose. I wonder if Mom will be mad forever. I hope not, but I wouldn't blame her.

I get up to find my Magic 8 Ball. I slide open my desk drawer. *Where is it?* I need some answers. I slam the drawer shut and tug the one underneath it open. It's not there, either. Then I remember last week, looking for Harry. I chucked it across the room. It wasn't very reliable...but maybe if I don't overload it with too many questions...if I ask it just *one*...I look under my dresser and feel a rush of relief. It's still there. But then I see the crack that zigzags across the plastic window. The liquid from inside the ball is gone. I see the blue stain in my carpet where it has leaked out. My Magic 8 Ball is broken. It's out of order. I can't go to it for answers anymore.

At first she doesn't see me. Mom is standing at the center island staring at an empty colander. A cutting board and knife lie in front of her, unused. When I slide the barn door closed she looks up.

"What are you doing in here, Jermaine?" My mother is angry.

"I want to help you make more relish for tomorrow," I say softly.

"Well, that's not possible," she says tersely. "I don't have any red bell peppers left to make the relish."

"Oh," I say. "What are you going to do?"

"That's a good question," she snaps. "What does one do when they need to create a new prize-winning product in less than twenty-four hours?" She rubs her eyes, then her cheeks, before she drops her hands and slumps against the counter, resting on her elbows and hanging her head.

"I'll help you," I tell her. Mom looks up at me.

"There's nothing to help with, Jermaine. I won't be able to participate in the Palooza contest." Mom carries the cutting board and knife over to the sink. She leans the board on its side against the basin. She opens a drawer and drops the knife inside. Then she unties her apron and folds it up, tossing it onto the countertop.

There has to be something we can come up with. Several jars of Mom's pickle products are set out on the work table. The little pickles in the sweet pickle mix remind me of fingers. It makes me think of Ro's lost ring. I feel a stab of panic. I push thoughts of the ring out of my mind. Instead I think about the things that go well with pickles, like hamburgers and ketchup. Hamburgers and ketchup lead to thoughts of other stuff you might like on your burger— tomatoes, onions, and lettuce, and other vegetables. Then all of a sudden these thoughts start smashing into each other...and there's that big tidal wave building up inside my head again. This time it's an idea for the pickle contest. Mom starts collecting the empty mason jars to put away.

"Wait!" I tell her. "Hold on!" I say excitedly.

"What now, Jermaine?" She sighs. "I'm tired. I want to go to bed."

"I have an idea!" I grap a jar of sweet pickles and a jar of pickled veggies.

"What are you doing?" Mom shouts. "Please, Jermaine," she whines, "I just cleaned up."

"One more second." I take one of the small onions and very carefully cut a hole through its center. I do the same with a carrot chunk. Then I stuff a small piece of pickle into each of the holes.

"Look! Your new product! Little Stuffers," I say, beaming. My mother's expression is completely blank. Then she shakes her head side to side. She opens her mouth to say something. My smile fades. She thinks it's a stupid idea.

"Jermaine," Mom says, "it's...it's...fantastic!" A huge smile lights up her face. Mom races around the barn. She pulls out a big pot and reaches for a ladle hanging on the wall. "I'll make the brine...I'm going to add cinnamon and ginger! When we're not in such a rush, we might add cauliflower and cherry peppers to the recipe. But this will do quite nicely."

Together, side by side, Mom and I chop, stuff, mix, and pour. It's almost midnight by the time the Little Stuffers are packed inside their jars. We slide them into the refrigerator. They will be all set in time for their debut at the Palooza tomorrow evening.

On our way back to the house I walk slightly behind my mother. The night is quiet except for the snow crunching under our boots.

"I'm sorry I knocked the table over," I tell her. My throat aches like a needle is sticking into my windpipe.

Mom doesn't answer. She keeps walking.

"I will never use my camera again." My voice shakes.

"I think you need a break from filming," she suggests.

"I wasn't very good at it anyways. Not good enough to be famous." I try to keep my voice steady and to stop the tears from spilling. But I can't. She stops and turns toward me. I see the moon's reflection in her eyes. A soft shine dances across her face. But the warm look she gives me, I know, comes from inside her. Her cold hand strokes my cheek.

"It takes time to be very good at something," she tells me. "You don't need to be famous so soon." Then Mom wraps her arms around me and pulls me in. Her jacket smells like winter and the pine hand lotion she keeps by the sink. I feel her breath in my hair and the gentle kiss she presses against my head. She holds me for a long time like that—long enough for me to realize that even without that skull ring, I am lucky.

"So you thought up a new idea for a pickle," Aunt Edie says proudly. She inflates balloons while Melinda hands them out.

"Yup," I say.

"Your Uncle Larry could learn a few tricks from you," she laughs.

"No hard feelings," Uncle Larry says, patting my head. Mom is chatting with Palooka customers while Zelda and I sit behind the table waiting to hand out samples. Dad arrives with a big carton of jars. "Here we go," he says, pulling out a couple of jars and topping off the pyramid, which has dwindled a bit. Then he slides the carton under the table with the rest of the stock. All of a sudden Zelda smacks my arm. I'm just about to smack her back when she whispers so no one can hear, "Look! There's a skull in one of the pickle jars." I slap my hand over my mouth like a person would do when they are totally surprised. At the very top of a pyramid, from inside a jar, the skull seems to smile at me through the glass.

"That's Ro's missing ring!" I whisper back. "How did that jar of dills end up here? They're not even pickled yet."

"How did Ro's ring end up inside it is the bigger question," Zelda says quietly.

Stay calm, I tell myself. I look around to make sure no one's paying attention. Before I can lift my arm to snatch the jar, Ro rushes up to the table.

"Hey!" she says to me.

"Ro! You're back from Florida. Did you have fun?" My eyes shift back and forth from Ro to the skull ring just inches away.

"It was a blast," she tells me. "Don't I have an awesome tan?" She pulls the neck of her shirt off her shoulder to show me her bathing-suit line.

"Wow," I say.

"Yeah, I know. I'm ready for my close-up in your reality show," she tells me.

"I'm not doing that anymore," I tell her.

"What? Why?" she asks.

"What?" Zelda interrupts. "You mean you annoyed everyone for nothing?" Ro's mom approaches the table.

"Hello, young ladies," she says. "What good workers you are. I will have to buy some of your mother's yummy pickles." She reaches up for the jar of dills. Before she can get her hand around it, my mother walks over to the table. She and the skull ring are practically eyeball to eyeball... if skulls actually *had* eyeballs. "How was your trip to Florida?" Mom asks.

"Ro's mom drops her arm and turns her back to me. "Wonderful, thank you. I was just about to buy some of your pickles." She whips around and reaches for the dills again.

"Wait!" I shout. "Try one of these first. Little Stuffers! They're brand-new! You're going to love them." I push the little sample up in her hand.

"Well, all right, Jermaine. Your mother is lucky to have such an enthusiastic helper." She takes the cup from my hand. "How delicious," she says, crunching away. "Do I taste a hint of ginger?"

"Ginger, it's in there!" My mother starts explaining about my idea for Little Stuffers. While they're distracted, I pluck the jar of dills from the pyramid, calmly whisking it under the table and grabbing another jar of dills for Ro's mom—making sure this one is actually pickled.

"Can I try a sample?" Ro asks.

"Sure," I say. Ro picks up a little cup of pickles. That's when I notice she's wearing the lucky skull ring on her finger!

"Hey!" I say. "How did you get that?"

"Before I left for Florida one of my brackets broke." Ro points to the braces on her front teeth. "I got another one out of the prize machine at the orthodontist's," she tells me matter-of-factly. Who would have guessed there was more than one lucky skull ring in this world? "You can keep my other one," she tells me. "It can be like our friendship ring."

After Ro and her mom leave, I tuck the dills inside my sweat shirt and sneak them into the bathroom. I have to dig around inside the jar a bit before I can finally reach the ring and pull it out. I munch through about half of the dills, which aren't very pickle-y yet, and then toss the rest into the garbage. Then I rinse the ring off and slide it onto my finger. If it was ever lucky to begin with, surely by now it's had all the good luck pickled out of it. I make a beeline back to the booth. I need to make sure there aren't any more of those un-pickled dills around. Only two other jars in the pyramid have a dated red sticker stuck to the bottom.

"What's going on?" my mother asks me.

"I think some of the jars got mixed up."

"How did that happen?" my mother asks. "How did *these* pickles get here?"

"You told me to bring extra dill pickles this morning," Dad explains.

"I told you to take the jars from the top shelves."

"I *did* take them from the top shelves...after I'd reorganized everything in the storage room."

"Reorganized?"

"There was no order to your pickles," said Dad. "So I moved all the dills together onto one shelf, all the sweet and spicy together...and everything is alphabetized now, starting with the bread and butters..."

"Clark!" my mother interrupts, "some of these pickles are not ready to sell. That's *why* we keep them on a separate shelf. Red sticker means not yet pickled!" Mom shows Dad the tiny red sticker with the date penciled on it. Dad's face lights up at the sight of it.

"Wow! Color-coded and dated! I'm impressed," he says.

"I'm just glad Jermaine caught the mistake before we sold any of those un-pickled dills. That would have been a a disaster," says Mom.

You have no idea, I'm thinking.

Later on in the evening, a voice booms over the loudspeaker.

"Ladddddddiiiiieeeesss and Gentlllllllemmen...piiiiickkkklllllle maaaaaakerrrrrrrs and piiiiickkkkklllllle looooverrrrrrrrs...THE JUDGES HAVE A WINNER...."

25
Almost Famous

"Hurry up, girls, we're waiting," Mom yells up from the kitchen.

"Coming," I shout back. Lying flat on my stomach, I continue to rub the carpet with the damp cloth. I can still see a tiny bit of the blue stain left from the Magic 8 Ball, but most of it is gone. Through the gap between the legs of my dresser, I notice Zelda's orange high-top sneakers in the doorway of my room.

"What are you doing down there?" she asks me.

"I spilled something and I'm trying to get it out," I explain. I give the carpet one last scrub before I inch my way up from the floor. That's when Zelda pulls something out from behind her back and gently tosses it onto my bed. It makes a soft thwack when it lands. My camera.

"Lose something?" she asks me. I smile. Not because I'm happy to see it, but because my sister cared enough to return it to me.

"Thanks," I tell her. Zelda almost smiles back, but catches herself.

"Whatever, dummy," she says.

Downstairs the Scrabble board is already set up on the kitchen table. This morning's *Bangor Daily News* article about the Palooza has been clipped out, each corner secured to the fridge with a magnet I collected yesterday from one of the other pickle-makers. Only the first-place winner got to have her picture taken, but Mom's name is listed with the other runner-up.

I play around with my Scrabble tiles for a few minutes before I spell the word *hockey*, to my father's delight. Zelda is building a small tower out of the unused tiles that are facedown in the center of the table.

"It's your turn," I remind her.

"*OH?* It's my turn," Zelda laughs as she places the letter *o* above the *h* in *hockey*.

"*O-K!*" she says, moving the *o* above the *k* instead. Then mom says, "Actually Zelda, that's very good. Your *o* is on the double word score square, which gives you a total of ten points!" Mom claps her hands cheerfully, and loud enough to startle Susie, who lifts up her head and barks.

"*Oh,* really?" Zelda giggles. That makes Mom laugh. Dad's turn is next. While he tries to spell out a word, my mother makes an announcement.

"Jermaine," she says, "what would you think if I put *your* face on the Little Stuffers label?"

"Are you kidding?" I practically scream. "*My* face is going to be on the label?"

"It was your idea," she tells me. "I can't take all the credit."

"Yes!" I shout. "I love that idea!" I can't believe it! My face is going to be on all the jars of Little Stuffers! My brain is thinking...photo shoot! And wondering about things like...national distribution! Now that Mom's business is expanding, and Little Stuffers won *first* runner-up... who knows where this will lead! My mind can't keep up with all the possibilities. I imagine my face smiling from the store shelves. *Hey, aren't you the pickle girl?* strangers will ask me. *I know you!* they'll point and say.

"Maybe I could be in a TV commercial?" I suggest.

"We'll have to sell *lots* of pickles before we can afford to do that," Mom tells me.

"I'm almost famous!" I yell.

"Almost..." Mom smiles.

"Almost..." I repeat.

26
Memories

"Granny, look into the camera," Nina says. I zoom in on Granny Viola's soft, wrinkled face. Mrs. Fairly sits next to her on one side and Nina is on the other.

"What do I do, again?" Granny V asks.

"Tell us stories about when you were younger. How you and Grandpa Keith met when you sat next to each other in the theater. And the year you lived in the city and sold hats at the fancy department store."

The nursing aides love my idea of filming the folks at the Bluebird Nest & Rest Senior Home. The video diaries will help some of the residents remember things they sometimes forget.

Pat helps me connect my video camera to the big TV. The residents, some in wheelchairs or holding walkers, some on their own frail legs, gather around the screen to watch themselves talk about their lives.

Mr. Chandler had a twin sister and grew up on a dairy farm. Mrs. Eggers wrote a book about good manners that was published. Mrs. Hopper sailed to Europe on a ship with her husband. Mr. Blakely has nine children, and six of them are doctors. When it's over, there's applause.

"Wonderful." Viola claps.

"Terrific!" Pat hoots. A warm flash of happiness spills over me.

"Take a bow, Jermaine!" Nina shouts above the cheers.

And I do.